7-10

BOOKS WRITTEN AND ILLUSTRATED BY
ROBERT LAWSON

BOOKS ILLUSTRATED BY
ROBERT LAWSON

Little, Brown and Company Books

MR. TWIGG'S MISTAKE

Mr. TWIGG'S MISTAKE

by
ROBERT LAWSON

LITTLE, BROWN AND COMPANY
BOSTON · 1947

*Printed simultaneously
in Canada by McClelland and Stewart Limited*

PRINTED IN THE UNITED STATES OF AMERICA

CONTENTS

The breakfast food herein mentioned is entirely fictitious. Any resemblance of "Bities" to any actual cereal, living or dead, is just unfortunate.

MR. TWIGG'S MISTAKE

Chapter 1

THE MAN OF SCIENCE

ALL THIS would never have happened if Mr. Twigg hadn't had a headache. Just why he had a headache has nothing to do with the case; that is entirely his affair, but he had one, a terrible one. He really shouldn't have tried to work that day, for he was not himself at all and his job was a most important one.

Mr. Twigg was the man who put the X Vitamins in Bita-Vita Breakfast Food (pronounced *Bite a Vita*) and the X Vitamins were the most important part of Bita-Vita, often called "Bities" for short. In fact the X Vitamins were about the only thing in Bities that did amount to much, the other ingredients being mostly toasted peanut shells, corn silk and coffee grounds (for that tangy, exotic, Pan-American flavor).

Every package of Bities contained no less than one hundred thousand units of the miraculous, growth-producing Vitamin X (this is what the advertisements said), that wonderful discovery which not only made you big and strong, but also imparted a sparkle to the eye, brought color to pale cheeks, eliminated freckles, made the teeth gleam, and improved the disposition, memory and figure.

It must have been very effective, for over eight hundred and seventy million packages of Bities were sold each year and they were eaten by most of the stars of stage, screen and radio, as well as the better baseball players, skating, tennis, Ping-pong and chess champions.

The advertisements also said that Bities were made in a most modern, sanitary factory, practically all windows, under the supervision of skilled scientists in spotless white. They showed nice, brightly colored pictures to prove it and these pictures in the magazines gradually made Mr. Twigg feel that he must be a skilled scientist, for, after all, he was the only one around the

4

place who had been through high school, and he did wear a white coat, although it was not always spotless. And he was the only one whose job was at all scientific; the others just shoveled or pushed hand trucks around in the packing department or worked in the offices.

So Mr. Twigg grew a little Vandyke beard like the scientists in the pictures and took to wearing glasses tied to a broad black ribbon. They came from the ten-cent store and he couldn't see very well with them on, but he always wore them on his way to and from work. He really looked quite distinguished and Mrs. Twigg was extremely proud of his appearance and of his high-class, scientific job. She even subscribed to the *Scientific American* and always kept a copy of it on the parlor table where visitors could see it and occasionally spoke of her husband as "*Dr. Twigg.*"

But on this particular morning he didn't feel at all distinguished or scientific; he just felt terrible. He came in, as usual, at exactly seven minutes to eight, hung his hat and coat and umbrella in his locker and put on his long white coat. Then he went into the washroom and took a couple of aspirins and a glass of water before sitting down at his machine. He looked at the clock, which said one minute to eight, and wished that it were one minute to eight on Sunday morning so that he could stay in bed, but it was only Tuesday so he had to go to work.

The machine that Mr. Twigg tended was a great big impressive affair. It consisted mostly of an enormous revolving drum like a huge concrete mixer. There were round chutes that came through the ceiling and went into the top of the drum and one fat pipe that came out of the bottom and went through the floor down to the packaging room. The machine was all enameled white with lots of shiny chromium knobs and wheels and levers and switches and dials. There was a clock over it with a big red second hand and in front of the control board was quite a comfortable chair where Mr. Twigg sat while working. His job might have seemed monotonous to some people, but because he felt it was scientific Mr. Twigg didn't mind it at all — when he didn't have a headache.

First he unlocked the steel vault where the valuable Vitamin X was kept in barrels. Then he dipped out a quart measure of the Vitamin, which looked about like uncooked oatmeal. He placed the measure on a scale and took out a little or added a little until it weighed exactly two and three-quarters pounds. This was the most scientific part of his job and Mr. Twigg did it very seriously, hoping that he looked like the pictures in the ads while doing so.

Next he opened a slide in the big drum and dumped in the Vitamins. He closed the slide, wrote a number on a chart and sat down in the comfortable chair. Then he pulled a lever which let one thousand pounds of the toasted peanut shells drop into the drum. Another lever added one hundred pounds of corn silk and still another added forty pounds of that exotic, tangy Pan-American flavoring (coffee grounds).

Then Mr. Twigg would look at the clock, turn a switch and the big drum would spin around at a high rate of speed, mixing the various things together or, as the advertisements said, *"blending these priceless ingredients to an indescribable perfection of golden, mellow, taste-appealing goodness."* It took exactly six minutes and thirty seconds to do this.

Mr. Twigg would now shut off the switch, bang three times on the fat pipe with a monkey wrench to let the packers know that the stuff was coming through, and pull another lever. This allowed the mixture to drop down the pipe to the packing machines, and since the drum contained enough Bities to fill six thousand eight hundred packages, it took almost half an hour for it to empty. While this was going on Mr. Twigg filled out his

7

charts and records, polished the chromium knobs, dials and levers and occasionally combed his neat Vandyke beard.

That was his usual routine, but this particular day, what with his headache and all the aspirin he'd taken, he was not at all scientific. He put in the Vitamin X all right and pulled all the levers correctly. But when it came to looking at the clock and turning on the switch that made the drum spin he slipped up badly. The electrically lighted clock with its big red second hand made him feel dizzy. He put his hand over his eyes and leaned back in the comfortable chair to rest a moment. When next he managed to focus on the clock six minutes and forty-five seconds had passed, so he hastily turned off the mixing switch, which he had never turned on, banged on the pipe and pulled the emptying lever. Then he went out to the washroom and took another aspirin.

Of course the Vitamin X, which had been dumped in first and had never been mixed with the other ingredients, slid down the pipe first and all of it went into the first package. So that one package was filled solidly with the powerful, undiluted Vitamin X, two and three-quarters pounds of it. The other packages from that batch were filled only with the toasted peanut shells, corn silk and coffee grounds as they came along, which didn't make much difference to anybody, but that first package did.

This particular box went through a packaging machine which inserted three circulars, a Bita-Vita Recipe Book, a premium coupon, a celluloid toy and two free tickets to the Bities Radio Hour. Then it was sealed in two layers of cellophane, making it dust- and moisture-proof, and practically impossible to open. Next it rolled along a conveyor, was counted by an electric eye and eventually was packed into a big carton along with twenty-three other packages that looked exactly the same but decidedly were not. The carton rolled along another conveyor, was sealed, stenciled, counted by another electric eye and finally stacked up in the shipping department where it stayed for a week or so.

On the following Tuesday this carton, along with several hundred others, was wheeled out onto the loading platform and packed into a freight car of the Chicago, Minneapolis and St. Paul Railroad. The car was numbered PX 48765321 and was one in a very long freight train. At Chicago the train was divided up and car No. PX 48765321 stood for several days on a siding next to the Stock Yards. It was fortunate that the packages of Bities were double-sealed with cellophane or they would have absorbed a tangy flavor and aroma that were not at all exotic or Pan-American.

Finally the car was put in another train which traveled over the tracks of the New York Central to Albany and from there over the Boston & Albany to the Bities District Warehouse at Hartford, Conn. Here all the cartons were unloaded and stacked up in the warehouse, where they remained for some time. During this wait a mouse got into one package and ate quite a few Bities, but as it went out of doors to die no great harm was done.

One bright spring day sixty or more cartons were loaded into a big, green trailer truck which had the name "Miss Lana T." painted on the front and was driven by a man named Salvatore Pondomi. Mr. Pondomi drove around all day, delivering cartons

of Bities to stores in Windsor Locks, Cross River, Branchville, South Hoosic, North Wendell and other places until along toward evening he pulled up at Charlie Keisler's market in Eastport. There was just one carton left and it was the one in which was that very exceptional package filled entirely with the powerful Vitamin X.

Of course Mr. Pondomi didn't know this and he wouldn't have done anything about it if he had known. So he just dumped the carton in the middle of the floor as usual, got the slip signed and helped himself to two bananas, a bunch of grapes, a marshmallow and a package of matches. Then he said, "Well, take it easy, Charlie," climbed into "Miss Lana T." tore the fenders off a couple of cars and drove back to East Hartford, where Mrs. Pondomi had a nice hot dinner waiting for him.

Charlie Keisler looked at the carton and said, "I suppose we ought to unpack it." He sighed deeply, for it was closing time and he was tired. Mrs. Keisler, who was extremely pretty but even more tired, said, "Oh, let Richard do it in the morning." So they pushed the carton in back of the counter, locked up the store and went home.

The next morning it just happened that the delivery car had a flat tire and Richard had to change that, so Mrs. Keisler had to unpack the Bities after all. This morning she had gotten all over being tired and was very brisk. In fact she was so brisk in putting the Bities boxes up on the shelves that she dropped several of them and it also just happened that one of them was that special box packed full of marvelous, powerful Vitamin X. This box fell into the basket containing Mrs. A. A. Appleton's order, which was all ready to be delivered.

Mrs. Keisler briskly gathered up the other boxes she had dropped, poked at her hair and went to answer the telephone, never noticing that particular, vitamin-packed box that had dropped into Mrs. Appleton's order. Richard finally got the tire changed, put adhesive tape on the knuckles he had skinned and delivered all his orders, including Mrs. Appleton's.

Pearlacy, the cook, picked up the box of Bities and asked Mrs. Appleton, who happened to be in the kitchen at the time, "Did you order these here?"

"Good Heavens, no," Mrs. Appleton answered. "Why would I?"

"I dunno," Pearlacy said. "Shall I send them back?"

"No, don't bother," Mrs. Appleton answered. "Just stick them on the shelf somewhere."

So Pearlacy stuck them up on a shelf somewhere and went on making a deep-dish apple pie, Mr. Appleton's favorite dessert.

Chapter 2

SQUIRT

ARTHUR AMORY APPLETON, more usually known as Squirt, was bored and lonesome. He had just returned from school for summer vacation, and while he loved his home and his parents it *was* rather quiet after the swarming life of boarding school. In a few days he would settle down and begin to

15

enjoy things, but at the moment he was being somewhat trying. In fact he was, according to his father's comments at breakfast, the White Man's Burden, a One-Boy Depression and a Perennial Pest.

He was walking across the lawn wishing there was something to do and someone to do it with, when he suddenly discovered both, in the form of a little gray, softly furred animal about the size of a mouse. At first he thought it was a field mouse, but then he noticed it was a different shape and didn't run away; it moved through the grass quite slowly, as though it were lost. He picked it up and it promptly bit him, not a bad bite, for its teeth, although sharp, were hardly large enough to penetrate the skin.

"Ouch," remarked Arthur Amory, shaking it off. This time he picked up the little creature with his handkerchief and ex-

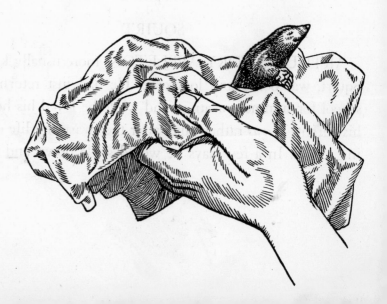

amined it more closely. It was cylindrical in shape with very short legs, the front ones equipped with large, flat feet turned outward. It had a pointed nose, practically no ears and its eyes were so small they were almost invisible. Its fur was short and delightfully soft.

Arthur Amory poked around in the tool house until he found a small cardboard box and put his find in that. It turned up its face as though trying to see him and kept opening its mouth. "It must be hungry," thought Squirt and went to consult his father.

He knew that Mr. Appleton would be busy in his writing room and that interruptions were strictly forbidden, but that didn't worry him especially. He went around the house, crossed the brick terrace and burst in without knocking, which was also forbidden.

"I bet you don't know what I've got," he announced.

"I know a great many things you've got," his father answered, taking off his glasses and scratching the bridge of his nose with them. "You've got the nerve of a Malay head-hunter, interrupting my work this way. You've got the manners of a gorilla, an untied shoestring and a smudge on your nose."

"It's a mole," said Squirt.

"I was not referring to your facial blemishes which are too many and too discouraging to think of," Mr. Appleton went on. "You have also got a long-suffering, infinitely patient parent who is about to break under the strain and commit braticide. If you have the rudiments of common sense, which I have good cause to doubt, you will remove yourself at once, before I take those fire tongs and break each and every bone in your loathsome young body."

"It seems to be quite a young one," Squirt said. "I think it may make a very interesting pet."

"Exactly what I thought when the nurse and doctor first displayed your infant hideousness to me. Never was a deluded parent more sadly disappointed; as an interesting pet you are a complete washout. I would much prefer a puff adder. They at least are clean, do not talk back and never open doors without knocking."

"I wonder what he eats," Arthur Amory said, looking in the box. "He seems to be hungry."

Mr. Appleton gingerly attempted to stroke the mole's head and was at once bitten. "I should judge," he said, sucking his forefinger, "that their first choice is human fingers. However,

RL

as I have a sentimental attachment for my own and as yours are far too grubby to offer to even the hungriest of moles, perhaps we had best seek some substitute. Fetch the encyclopedia — Vol. 15, MARY to MUS — and *don't* trip over the lamp cord.

"Here we are," he muttered, poring over the heavy book, "Molasses — Mold — Moldavice — *Mole* — a small animal of the family *Talpidae* (that's helpful). Hm — Golden mole — Asiatic zokors (I thought that was a movie clan). Australian marsupial family — Here we have it — *the food of the mole consists chiefly of worms and grubs.* Well, that settles it. I had always wondered what earthly use little boys were to man or nature and there's your answer, mole food. Miserable worms and grubs that they are — "

"It says here," said Squirt, reading over his father's shoulder, "that the mole is a voracious eater. Maybe there's some of that in the pantry."

"I doubt it," sighed Mr. Appleton. "I seem to recollect hearing on the radio that the voracious factory was destroyed some weeks ago, by an earthquake."

"Well, he's got to have *something,*" said his son. "It says that if deprived of food it will succumb in ten to twelve hours."

"That is a simple solution," Mr. Appleton said. "Merely deprive it of food for twelve hours and we will not have to worry further. I wonder if pestiferous brats could be disposed of in the same easy manner? I shall propose it to your mother."

20

"No," said Squirt.

"Very well, there is another alternative. The encyclopedia states that moles take readily to water (unlike certain people I could name). You might, if so disposed, walk down the hill to the brook, stand in the exact center of the bridge and drop this bloodthirsty brute into the raging torrent. If he takes readily to water all well and good; if not you have my permission to try the same experiment on your own dear self. I will cheerfully pay the expense of having the brook dragged and the bodies recovered. I might even — "

"No," said Squirt.

"As usual, my advice is spurned. Then the only answer I can see is that you devote the rest of your young life to digging worms and grubs, a dull occupation, but one doubtless well suited to your almost non-existent mentality. Kindly carry on your excavations at some point on the premises as far as possible removed from this window — and begin them at once."

"It's started to rain," his son objected.

Mr. Appleton glanced out of the window and groaned. "So it has — briskly. I must, for once, confess myself stumped. Put back the encyclopedia — and mind that lamp cord."

Squirt replaced the book and avoided tripping over the lamp cord, but did manage to dislodge a stack of magazines. As they cascaded to the floor his father's eye was caught by a brightly colored advertisement on the back cover of one.

"Eureka!" he shouted. "Our problem is solved, or practically solved. There is your answer. *Bita-Vita, the Universal Taste Thrill!* Observe that it is the favorite food of practically every prominent person in these United States. Note the photograph of the beautiful lady, Miss Patricia Van der Doncken Cadwallader-Smythe, aristocratic, brilliant, cultured, studious (that's why she's shown in a bathing suit) and *devoted* to Bities. If they are good enough for her they are certainly good enough for this lowly creature you insist on preserving. Give him Bities at once.

"And on your way to the kitchen you will kindly tell your mother that when Mr. Draper of the *Times* telephones, inquiring after this article which I am supposedly writing, she may inform him that Mr. Appleton's work has been greatly delayed by the stupid interruptions of his imbecile son."

"I don't think we have any Bities, anyway," said Arthur Amory, taking his departure.

However, when he asked in the kitchen Pearlacy promptly produced the box which had arrived only the day before, that special box which Mr. Twigg's headache had caused to be filled with pure, undiluted Vitamin X.

"Did your ma say you could have these?" she asked.

"No," said Squirt, "but father told me to feed some to this very interesting little animal I found. It is a mole, a small animal of the family *Talpidae*. I am going to tame it. I think it will make a very interesting pet."

"He don't look interesting," Pearlacy said, looking in the box. "All he do is open his mouth."

"He's hungry," Squirt explained. "If deprived of food for ten to twelve hours he will succumb."

"You don't say." Pearlacy received the information with little enthusiasm. "Well, he ain't going to do any succumbing in my kitchen. Take him out to the tool house."

23

"I expect to," said Squirt. "I am going to teach him to do some very interesting tricks. His name is de Gaulle. I have named him that because General de Gaulle was head of the French underground movement and moles are underground animals. I also thought of calling him John L. Lewis, because John L. Lewis is head of the miner's union and moles are sort of miners, but it's not a very interesting name."

"I'd call him St. Lucien Beauregard if he was mine," suggested Pearlacy. "That's a real pretty name."

"It's pretty, but not very interesting. Is there any chocolate cake?"

"Lord!" she sighed, reaching for the cake box. "And not two hours sence your breakfast. I suppose was you deprived of food mor'n two hours you'd do whatever that was you just said."

"Succumb?" said Squirt. "I probably would because I've had a very busy morning. Thank you very much. Come along, de Gaulle."

In the tool house with the aid of a pruning knife and the asparagus cutter Arthur Amory managed to remove the cellophane covering and get the Bities package open. He took out a pinch of the soft oatmeal-like flakes and placed them in the mole's box. De Gaulle was distinctly interested. He approached,

sniffed, sneezed, backed away, circled and advanced several times before finally venturing to eat one flake. He shivered slightly, ate one more and then crouched, his mouth open, panting.

"I guess he's thirsty," Squirt thought. He found a small saucer, filled it with water and placed it in the box. The mole lapped eagerly, his narrow tongue moving like lightning. Then he wiped his mouth with his broad forepaws, stretched a few times, curled up and went to sleep. Every once in a while his body jerked and quivered as though he were dreaming.

There were a few flakes of uneaten Bities, so Squirt wet his finger, picked them up and tasted them. They didn't taste like much, slightly mouldy and a bit like sulphur. He found a handful of raffia and covered up the sleeping General. Then he read the various circulars and the Bities recipe book.

The warm rain drummed steadily on the low shingle roof. Arthur Amory stretched out on a couple of bags of fertilizer and also took a nap.

Interesting
Tricks, I have
taught General
De Gaulle. Mole.
(Family Talpidae)
#1. T5....

Chapter 3

THE BOOK OF TRICKS

AT DINNER that night Mr. Appleton observed to Mrs. Appleton, "Your son seems to resemble the perfect hoodlum rather more than usual this evening. Is it mere slovenliness which causes his collar to be unbuttoned or is that the latest fashion among the younger set?"

"It's too tight," said Arthur Amory, finishing his second helping of deep-dish apple pie.

"One may also note," his father continued, "an extraordinary expanse of wrist protruding beyond a pair of not-too-clean cuffs.

I had always considered that the leg of an ostrich exhibited the most revolting area of skin to be found anywhere in nature, but I am now forced to the conclusion that a pair of well-chapped boys' wrists are even more unappetizing."

"Amie, pull down your sleeves," said Mrs. Appleton.

"They're too short," said Squirt, struggling with them and upsetting a fingerbowl.

"Stand up," ordered his father.

Arthur Amory did so and it was at once apparent that his coat sleeves were far too short and his collar entirely too tight.

"Good Heavens," said Mrs. Appleton. "That is your best suit and it was perfectly all right Sunday when we went to church. Whatever have you done to it?"

"Go over to the door," his father said.

Arthur Amory dutifully went over and stood straight up with his back against the door jamb where his measurements were recorded. The last mark had been made only four days before, on his return from school, but now, when Mr. Appleton carefully tried it with a book his head towered at least an inch and a half above the last line. After marking it and penciling some hasty calculations his father sighed, "Well, this *is* the last straw. One and one-half inches in four days means three-eighths of an inch per day. At that rate the hundred days of vacation which we are unhappily facing will add approximately thirty-seven inches to the height of our cherished offspring. Therefore, at the sum-

mer's end we shall possess a creature some seven feet eight inches tall. His present four feet eight is exactly four feet too much to view with any equanimity; the prospect of three feet more of the same is horrifying."

"Nonsense, Arthur," Mrs. Appleton said. "You never could add. Run along, Amie, and do put some cold cream on your hands."

"It may be the Bita-Vita I ate that's made me grow," Squirt suggested. "I read a very interesting booklet in the box that said each package contained one hundred thousand units of the miraculous, growth-producing Vitamin X. I only ate a tiny bit, because it tasted nasty, but General de Gaulle seemed to like it — "

"Don't tell me they've gotten a testimonial from *him*," exclaimed Mr. Appleton.

"General de Gaulle," Arthur Amory explained, "is the very interesting little mole I showed you this morning. You advised me to feed him Bita-Vita. I am making a pet of him and I expect to teach him some very interesting tricks."

"As a teacher of tricks you should rate highly," his father remarked, "although I cannot imagine them being in the least interesting. Where is the brute?"

"Up in my room," Squirt answered. "I have made him a bed in an old shoebox filled with raffia. He seems to sleep a great deal, but I think that is because he is growing so fast. He is almost twice as large as he was this morning. That Vitamin X in Bities must be very powerful."

"It must be," Mr. Appleton agreed, ruefully eying his son's protruding wrists. "If you dare eat another flake of it I shall be forced to hang you up by the thumbs and flay you alive. Go to bed."

Arthur Amory kissed his parents and went up to his room where he found General de Gaulle wide awake and quite lively. His mouth was open, so Squirt gave him a few flakes of Bities. He only ate two, which seemed to be his limit, then lapped up half a saucer of water, washed his face and paws thoroughly, burrowed into the raffia and went to sleep. He certainly was growing rapidly; he was now almost as large as a chipmunk and as Squirt watched him, twitching and occasionally turning in his sleep, it almost seemed as though he grew larger by the moment.

Arthur Amory found a school exercise book and on the first blank page wrote:

INTERESTING TRICKS I HAVE TAUGHT GENERAL
DE GAULLE. Mole (Family *Talpidae*)

#*1.* *To eat Bities.*
#*2.* *To wash his face and paws after eating.*
#*3.* *To grow rapidly.*
#*4.* *Not to bite me.*

He really should not have claimed full credit for all of these accomplishments, for the General had done most of them of his own free will, but this was too fine a point to worry over and Squirt was soon sleeping as soundly as his pupil.

Downstairs Mrs. Appleton said, "Goodness, I hope he doesn't smell — General de Gaulle, I mean."

Mr. Appleton, who was reading, answered absently, "Of

course he does, all Frenchmen do — pomade, brilliantine, Eau de Cologne — "

"I mean the mole, silly."

"Oh, the mole. Well, he will too. If he doesn't it will be the first time that any of our darling child's nature enthusiasms has not been accompanied by a nauseous, charnel-house odor. Horned toads, white mice, turtles, pollywogs, and that tropical aquarium — phew! I have never been able to bear clam chowder since *that* episode. Why is it that every activity of little boys should result in either an outlandish racket or a horrible smell?"

His wife sniffed the air. "Speaking of smells," she announced placidly, "your vest is on fire again. You really must be more careful with that old pipe, Arthur."

It turned cool sometime before morning and Squirt woke enough to pull up his blanket. When he wakened fully, sometime later, he became conscious of a snug sensation of comforting warmth. Reaching up he discovered the soft form of General de Gaulle draped around his neck.

"Goodness, General," he cried, picking him up. "You've grown terrifically during the night." He had indeed, for he was now fully as large as a gray squirrel. His short fur was delightfully soft and smooth. Squirt stroked it and de Gaulle, smiling pleasantly, licked his hand, then squirmed around and began on his left ear. It tickled unbearably and Squirt sprang up and

washed and dressed himself while the mole curled up on the still warm pillow.

He was given his two flakes of Bities and while he washed his face and paws Squirt got out the exercise book and wrote down:

#5. *To act as a muffler (a very useful trick).*
#6. *To lick my hands.*

Then he went down to his own breakfast.

All that week General de Gaulle's growth and training proceeded at a rapid pace. Arthur Amory quickly lost his lonesomeness and boredom and became completely engrossed in his new-found companion. They were together constantly, out and about all day long. Mr. Appleton's privacy was seldom invaded;

even raids on the cakebox became so infrequent that Pearlacy became worried about Mr. Squirt's appetite.

The "List of Interesting Tricks" now occupied two full pages of the exercise book and was added to daily. On the first day the General began to dig and his prowess in this soon became phenomenal. He would place his broad forepaws together over his head, give a slight wiggle and slide into the ground as easily and smoothly as a diver entering the water.

Squirt taught him to stay well below the surface, for with his rapidly increasing size, had he burrowed just under the sod in the usual manner of moles the lawn and garden would soon have become a shambles.

They developed any number of games based on a sort of sub-surface hide and seek. De Gaulle would dig down and Arthur Amory would race about the hillside, sometimes running noisily, sometimes sneaking on tiptoe. Then he would sit down quietly and no matter how far or how fast he had run, within a few minutes there would be a slight stirring of the ground and a gentle nip on the ankle as the mole heaved himself up out of the ground, panting and grinning triumphantly.

This game lent itself to many variations. Sometimes de Gaulle was a band of gallant Union prisoners tunneling their way out of Libby Prison. Squirt, his ear pressed to the ground, would attempt to locate the sound and thwart the escape. Since this was rather hard on the ears, an improvement was soon con-

33

cocted consisting of a tin can with a small hole cut in the bottom.

This highly unscientific device, christened a Super-Radar-Sonotonoscope, was also used when de Gaulle, as an enemy submarine, vainly tried to elude a barrage of depth bombs, indicated by heavy whacks of a spade. According to the rules when one thumped directly above the enemy he must come to the surface and roll on his back in imitation of the helpless submarine wallowing in a trough of the sea. The *coup de grâce* was administered by tickling the softly furred gray stomach, which threw the doomed sub into a highly realistic death flurry.

There were many other games and accomplishments to be entered in the copybook. Learning to stand on his head was nothing at all for the General. His great shovel-shaped forefeet and stout bowed arms made an unexcelled base and he could remain upright indefinitely. With less ease and considerable coaching he even succeeded in scrambling about in the lowest branches of the apple tree, a feat duly recorded in the Book of Tricks as:

#17. To be the only tree climbing Mole in the Younivers.

De Gaulle appeared to enjoy all these pastimes greatly and was most amiable and versatile, assuming the role of Moby Dick, Jules Verne's *Nautilus* or an escaping prisoner with equal zest and good humor. One thing that astonished Squirt and caused him some slight envy was the fact that the General al-

ways emerged from these subterranean expeditions with his fur and paws cleaner than ever; no sign of earth ever clung to him. Moreover he did not, as Mrs. Appleton had feared, smell. About his person there was just that faint and indescribable aroma that is one of the endearing features of young kittens. This pleasant scent was the first thing that Squirt was conscious of on awakening each morning, for despite his rapidly increasing bulk de Gaulle still persisted in his habit of arriving sometime during the night and draping himself on his playmate's chest.

Arthur Amory chose a rather unfortunate moment to comment on this exceptional cleanliness of the family *Talpidae,* for it had been a dampish day and a whole wolf pack of Nazi submarines had been annihilated, so despite the aid of the Super-Radar-Sonotonoscope he had acquired a heavy coating of mud, pine needles and other foreign matter. All of which gave Mr. Appleton the pleasant opportunity for a fifteen-minute lecture on the filthiness of little boys in general and his son in particular.

The General's amazing growth became a matter of some concern, for by the end of the week he had attained the size of a Belgian hare and his bed had been enlarged from the original shoebox to a wooden soapbox. His diet still consisted of only two flakes of Bities three times per day and innumerable saucers of water. This much seemed to satisfy him completely, but mystified everyone else.

"There is," Mr. Appleton said, "something distinctly screwy about this. A creature of this size could not possibly sustain itself on six flakes of that horrible stuff per day, to say nothing of growing at the speed of Juvenile Delinquency."

"You've never eaten it," Mrs. Appleton observed. "It may be very nourishing; the advertisements say it is."

"I have indeed sampled it," he retorted. "Two years ago on a Pullman diner while passing through the outskirts of Lorain, Ohio. The waiter brought me a dish of it by mistake. I remember the occasion distinctly for at the moment I was wondering if anywhere in the world there could be anything more dismal than the outskirts of Lorain, Ohio, and on tasting this drab muck promptly decided that there was — Bities. Believe it or not, Bities are even more unappetizing than the outskirts of Lorain, Ohio, on a rainy November morning and moreover there is not enough nourishment in a truckload of it to sustain a ladybug for an hour."

"Oh well, perhaps General de Gaulle is just naturally a big mole," she said.

"A *big mole*," he snorted. "My dear, do you realize that the largest mole ever known to science (I've been reading up on them) measured just under eleven inches in length and weighed some forty-seven ounces. I do not know just what that amounts to in pounds, without a pencil, but I'm sure it is not one-fourth the size and weight of this amiable monstrosity which we have acquired. This cannot possibly be a mole, yet there is nothing else it possibly can be."

"Nonsense," said Mrs. Appleton. "Of course he's a mole and a very nice one, too, aren't you, de Gaulle, even if you are a bit oversize?" She stroked the head of the General, who smiled broadly and licked her fingers. "Anyway, Amory is coming out tomorrow for the week end and he will know all about it."

"I will admit that your brother, in addition to being the very worst bridge player in the world, is one of its most distinguished naturalists. If anyone could throw light on this weird mystery he should be that one, but I doubt if even he can, and his bridge game will certainly be the worse for it, if one can imagine such a thing."

"Oh, good," said Squirt. "I didn't know Uncle Amory was coming out. I'm glad, because he always brings me something very interesting. Of course I like him anyway, but I like him even more when he brings me something nice. Come along, de Gaulle; let's learn a new trick for Uncle Amory."

Pearlacy was the only one who was not perturbed by the General's growth. Never having seen an ordinary mole she was not particularly impressed by his size. Moreover, she was engrossed in the problem of whether to have deep-dish apple pie or chocolate soufflé for tomorrow night's dinner.

"Your Pa just loves his deep-dish pie," she said, "but yo' Uncle Amr'y certainly is partial to chocolate soofle."

Squirt absorbed a slab of cocoanut layer cake while debating the problem. "Why don't we have both?" he suggested. "What do you think, de Gaulle?"

De Gaulle smiled pleasantly and licked his chops. "You see," said Squirt, "he says yes."

"He certainly is cute," said Pearlacy, cutting another slice of cake, "but I wish you'd named him St. Lucien Beauregard."

"Maybe I will," Squirt agreed, accepting the bribe. "General St. Lucien Beauregard de Gaulle would be a very interesting name."

"It certainly would look handsome on a marriage certificate or something," said Pearlacy. "Real handsome."

Chapter 4

UNCLE AMORY

THEY WENT DOWN in the station wagon to meet Uncle
Amory and Squirt was not disappointed, for his uncle bore an
oddly shaped package which he thrust at him, saying testily,
"Here Squirt, take this, take this, something for you, hope you
like it, ought to, ought to. Yes, yes, fine, fine, fine."

Uncle Amory was a short little man, not much taller than Squirt. He was quite bald and his round pink face, had it not been for his glasses, would have given the impression of a rather fretful baby. His movements were always quick and sudden and his speech came in short, rapid bursts, like a balky outboard motor. He did not look at all like one of the world's foremost scientists, although he really was.

"Hello, Helen," he now cried. "Looking splendid, splendid, nice of you to come down. Arthur, splendid, splendid, good to see you. Warm, confoundedly warm, well, well, well. What are we waiting for?"

"We are waiting," said Mr. Appleton, lighting his pipe, "for: item one: you to finish your imitation of an hysterical homecoming college girl and get into the car; item two: for your imbecile nephew to stop trying to open that package and retrieve your bag, over which three persons have so far tripped; item three —"

"Fine, fine, splendid," Uncle Amory said, settling himself. He removed his hat and vigorously polished his shining pink dome of forehead with a large silk handkerchief. "Had to go out to Nebraska last week. Another degree, getting to be a nuisance, this degree business. Hot there, deucedly hot. Two lectures and a dinner in Chicago; hot there too. Worn out. Looking forward to a good quiet game of bridge. Have a new system (Mr. Appleton groaned). That's an arrow, Squirt; hope you'll enjoy it;

knew you were a great toxophilite. See that you don't lose it, confoundedly expensive. Ridiculous. That idiotic clerk — "

"*An* arrow — one *arrow?*" queried Mr. Appleton. "What possible, earthly use is *one* arrow? One straw in a haystack, one drop in a bucket. Why, this young vandal consumes arrows faster than I do cigarettes. Every time I go to the village for tobacco I bring him back a dozen arrows and they're gone before I've opened my second pack. The last one disappeared yesterday, I believe, on the garbage truck, either in, or close to, the seat of Mr. Enoch Swain's overalls."

"It wasn't quite the last one; I still have four left," Arthur Amory corrected. "Anyway, it was all Enoch's fault. I warned him that the Deadwood Coach was going to be ambushed down on the curve in the drive and that he'd better submit quietly, but he decided to make a run for it, so I let him have it."

"The 'run for it' resulted in quite a trail of scattered garbage and trash down the driveway," Mrs. Appleton reminded him, "as well as the lost arrow. Never mind, Enoch will bring it back Monday, *if* he comes back Monday."

"It was that fool clerk's fault," Uncle Amory exploded. "Silly, supercilious young pup. Went into Abercrombie's and said I wanted some arrows for a nephew. 'Just what quality?' says this young snip, superior as the Devil. 'Why, the best, of course,' I said. 'My nephew, you know, named after me, must have the best, naturally.' So he dawdled around and finally spread these

out. 'These are $48 the dozen,' he said; *the* dozen, mind you —
'plus tax.' Preposterous! 'I'll take *one,*' I said. Sound like a fool
asking for a cheaper sort. 'Just one, and see that you wrap it carefully.' Took the idiot fifteen minutes to get that done — almost
missed my train. Then he says, 'That will be $4 — plus tax.'
Damned nonsense, preposterous price, rank racketeering. Going
to write a letter to the *Times.* Hope you like it, Amory; ought
to be good."

"I shot an arrow into the air," murmured Mr. Appleton, "four
bucks went, I know not where — plus tax."

By this time Squirt had managed to open one end of the package and draw out the arrow. It *was* a beauty, clerk or no clerk.
It was slender and light, perfectly balanced, mahogany-footed,
the nock reinforced with ebony. The varnish was rubbed to a
satiny finish, it was marked with brilliant stripes of red, blue and
gold and the cock feather was a glowing orange. Squirt, for once,
was speechless with awe and admiration.

"Oh, Uncle Amory," he finally gasped, "it's the most beauti-
ful arrow I've ever owned. I've never had anything but quarter
ones, except two fifty-centers that Aunt Addie gave me. I think
I will name it Excalibur, or perhaps Daniel Boone. Wait until
General de Gaulle sees it, I know he'll be excited. General de
Gaulle is my pet mole, you know, and I'm sure you'll like him.
He's a very interesting pet."

"Mole — de Gaulle, de Gaulle?" popped Uncle Amory. "Al-

43

ways looked more like an anteater to me — or a llama. De Gaulle, eh? Well, well, well."

"I have named him General de Gaulle," Squirt explained, "because General de Gaulle was head of the underground movement and moles are underground animals. I have taught him some very interesting tricks. I've taught him a new trick, especially for you."

"You don't say, you don't say," cried Uncle Amory heartily. "De Gaulle, eh, well, well, well, splendid, splendid. Now, Arthur, this new bidding system. I learned it from some people in Denver. It works like this — "

Mr. Appleton moaned heavily and narrowly avoided side-swiping Mr. Swain's garbage truck, while Arthur Amory, recognizing the Deadwood Coach, leaned out and emitted a series of bloodcurdling Apache war whoops.

Squirt's parents and Uncle Amory were on the terrace enjoying tall, cool drinks, when General de Gaulle was brought around to be introduced. The General, by now, was fully as large as a large woodchuck, different in shape, of course, but about that bulk.

Uncle Amory was deep in an explanation of his new bidding system and paid little attention at first, but when de Gaulle displayed his latest Interesting Trick, which consisted of standing on his head and balancing a tennis ball on his hind feet, the

scientist gradually began to take in that this large creature was
what Squirt had been referring to as a mole.

He put down his glass with great care and pushed it across the table, well out of reach. His last sentence halted in the middle and drifted into silence. His eyes bulged slightly.

"This is General de Gaulle, Uncle Amory," said Squirt, "my pet mole that I was telling you about, and this is his latest trick that I have taught him especially for you." He stamped twice on the ground and the General spun the tennis ball with his hind feet, then kicked it up in the air. Squirt caught it and de Gaulle did a back flip and sat up, smiling pleasantly.

"Great Caesar's ghost!" Uncle Amory gasped. He removed his glasses with slightly shaking hands, polished them carefully and put them back on, peered sharply at the General, at Squirt and then at the landscape as though testing his sight. "*A mole!*" he whispered. "A mole, family *Talpidae*. Preposterous! Absurd!"

He turned suddenly on his brother-in-law and burst out, "Arthur, what did you put in that drink? This is perfectly impossible; things like this do not happen. Don't you people realize that the largest mole ever recorded measured under eleven inches in length and weighed only forty-seven ounces? It was — "

"I know," Mr. Appleton replied. "It was found by Von Schmiddle, in New Caledonia in 1903. It is now stuffed and reposes in the Smithsonian. I have been reading up on moles and only recently remarked to my charming wife, your sister,

46

that this amiable monstrosity cannot possibly be a mole — yet there is nothing else it possibly can be."

"Shake hands with Uncle Amory, General," Squirt ordered. De Gaulle obediently waddled over, sat up and extended a broad paw. Uncle Amory gingerly shook it and then examined it carefully, top, bottom and sides. In a dazed silence he leaned forward, studying the softly furred head, checking each feature. The General smiled amiably and licked the inquiring fingers.

Uncle Amory suddenly reached for his glass and finished its contents in one gulp. "Helen," he said, a little shakily, "I think I'd best take a short rest before dinner. I must be overtired. I do not feel quite myself." He wandered away dazedly, while Squirt and General de Gaulle went to try out the new arrow, which had now been definitely christened Excalibur.

The nap and dinner somewhat restored Uncle Amory's nerves, although he was still too upset to attempt bridge, a fact which put Mr. Appleton in a most genial mood and caused him to beam on the General with the greatest affection. Uncle Amory spent much of the evening questioning Squirt on de Gaulle's diet, habits, etc. and was given an exhibition of all the Interesting Tricks except those which involved digging. The living room being unsuited to these they were held over for the next day.

"Of course I shall have to do a Paper on this," Uncle Amory said. "It will take several days so I'm afraid I will have to ask you to stretch your hospitality through most of next week. I shall also have to have Fulton out for a day to take photographs and Miss Finney for a day or so to make drawings. I am afraid I shall be a great nuisance, Helen, but this is one of the most remarkable occurrences in a decade. It's unbelievable, really, perfectly preposterous, yet it *seems* to be true."

"Of course it's true," Mrs. Appleton said, scratching de Gaulle's head, "and it's nice that you can make a real visit. Perhaps we can work in some bridge after all."

This thought drew a glare from Mr. Appleton who, however, added his cordial invitation and Squirt cried, "Oh that's fine, Uncle Amory. We can play Libby Prison and I'll teach you to use the Super-Radar-Sonotonoscope. Come along, de Gaulle, it's past bedtime."

The next day, which was Sunday, Uncle Amory rested a great deal, recovering from his Western trip and from the previous day's surprise, also planning his Paper on this phenomenon. While he showed a satisfactory appreciation of de Gaulle's digging prowess and outdoor tricks, murmuring, "Remarkable, remarkable, very clever, very clever indeed," his mind was really engrossed with the General's spectacular size and amazing growth.

"The most incredible of all the impossible things about the animal," he kept repeating, "is the diet. Why, a mouse could not exist on six flakes per day of that miserable trash. It's preposterous, absurd — yet he does."

"Perhaps he eats something when he is underground, turnips or something," suggested Mrs. Appleton.

"More likely he visits the nearby graveyard," her husband said, "and absorbs the vigor of our hardy pioneer ancestors."

"Perhaps he eats atoms; they are very powerful," Squirt volunteered.

Uncle Amory went off and took another nap.

On Monday, however, he set to work with energy and determination and put Squirt and the General through a long, tiring day. De Gaulle was measured, calipered and examined from every angle. His blood pressure was taken, his nervous reactions noted, he was weighed at hourly intervals. His drinking water

RL

was analyzed and measured and his pulse read before and after each meal. Uncle Amory bustled around as actively as an Aberdeen terrier, making notes, long-distance telephone calls and invading Mr. Appleton's writing room to borrow paper or use the typewriter. He was not particularly interested in the Super-Radar-Sonotonoscope and there was no time at all to play Libby Prison.

Squirt found scientific research rather wearing and while refreshing himself with a slab of chocolate cake and a glass of milk confided to Pearlacy, "Uncle Amory is a very interesting naturalist and my favorite uncle, but he certainly has kept St. Lucien Beauregard and me going hard today."

"Ain't he an active gentman?" Pearlacy agreed. "He shore does busy around. Certainly has got hisself excited over a little old mole."

"General de Gaulle is the very biggest mole in the entire whole world," Squirt replied with dignity. "He's a very interesting pet and very intelligent. Uncle Amory says he's a phenomenon."

"You don't say," Pearlacy said, starting a new deep-dish apple pie, "and all this time you've been telling me he was a mole."

On Tuesday Mr. Fulton arrived with a carload of cameras and photographic equipment. The General was photographed in every possible position, from every possible angle. He was photographed lying down beside a yardstick and standing up beside a yardstick, from above, in front, behind and underneath. There were movie action shots showing him standing on his head, climbing in the apple tree, digging, and imitating a whale's death flurry. There were pictures of him eating, drinking, washing his face, scratching himself and washing Squirt's ear. There

were pictures of him in Squirt's arms, on Uncle Amory's lap, being petted by Mrs. Appleton and shaking hands with Mr. Appleton. Mr. Fulton even obligingly took a picture of Pearlacy to send to her aunt in South Carolina.

As a reward for his co-operation Squirt was presented with a whole basketful of used flashlight bulbs which would make splendid targets for testing the accuracy of Excalibur when and if he ever found time for archery.

Wednesday and Thursday were devoted to Miss Finney, who made innumerable beautifully accurate watercolors of de Gaulle and various details of his anatomy, while Squirt breathed heavily on her neck and offered suggestions and criticisms.

On Friday Uncle Amory's secretary, Miss Poulter, arrived, bearing numerous reference books and departed with a great sheaf of notes to transcribe and type. Saturday the note making, measurements and tests continued. During the week the General's length had increased by slightly over four inches and his weight by some forty-eight ounces. Sunday Uncle Amory rested and on Monday he took his departure, eager to get back to the Museum and complete his report.

On Sunday he had suggested that, in the interest of science, de Gaulle should be sent in to the safekeeping of the Zoo, a proposal which met with an immediate and firm negative. Squirt's refusal took the form of a loud, siren-like bellow as he gathered his pet in his arms and fled up the hill to the refuge of the pine

wood. Mrs. Appleton's reaction was less spectacular, but equally decided.

"Why, Amory," she cried. "The very idea. De Gaulle belongs to Amie and he's going to stay right here, I wouldn't dream of having him in any smelly old Zoo. I'm surprised at your even thinking of such a silly thing."

"Sorry, sorry," Uncle Amory sputtered. "Really belongs to science, but of course, of course. Shouldn't have suggested it. Arthur, run up and tell him I'm sorry."

Mr. Appleton managed to locate and reassure Squirt, and de Gaulle, who had taken refuge deep underground, was persuaded to come to the surface.

"General," said Mr. Appleton, bowing deeply. "Do you realize that due entirely to you and your burning interest to science the word 'bridge' has not even been mentioned one single time during the week just past? Would that I were empowered to bestow on you the Medal of Merit, the Legion of Honor, The Golden Star of Persia, with palms, or even a beefsteak, with mushrooms. In lieu of these pray accept my eternal thanks, devotion and gratitude."

General de Gaulle smiled pleasantly, bit him on the ankle and they all raced each other down the hill.

Chapter 5

EXCALIBUR

AT LAST Squirt had time to really try out Excalibur and it proved to be as superior in performance as it was in looks. All the flashlight bulbs were soon demolished, for the four old, shabby, twenty-five cent arrows, seemingly inspired by their elegant new comrade, turned in remarkable performances. Soon, in the best tradition of Robin Hood, Squirt was reduced to using a peeled willow wand as a mark. It really made a most satisfactory target, for though one seldom hit it, it was easy to come quite close and the misses always seemed a little closer than they really were. General de Gaulle, temporarily Friar Tuck, was enjoying the sport and taking an occasional trip underground, when the unfortunate incident occurred.

Squirt really should not have been shooting down in that corner of the south field anyway, because it was dangerously close to Mr. Snarple's garden and there had already been several slight unpleasantnesses. One had to do with a broken glass in the Snarple greenhouse, another concerned a cold frame. These were both Squirt's fault which he freely admitted and for which he had made full payment.

The unpleasantness was all the result of Mr. Snarple's failure to understand the temperamental behavior of arrows, his refusal to believe that these incidents were not deliberate deviltry — and his angry smashing of the arrows involved. He had also used some very unfortunate language and had implied that many other depredations could be traced to his young neighbor, which was entirely untrue. The real trouble was that he was just a thoroughly unpleasant, suspicious and nasty little man, "the meanest white gentman I ever *did* see," as Pearlacy expressed it.

Mr. Appleton's opinion was more elaborate and included such

descriptive phrases as "preposterous little popinjay," "frustrated Cockney twerp" and many others, adding the dark conviction that Mr. Snarple bought his clothes from the Swellfello Men's Shoppe, his liquor from hijackers and his cigars from the cleaning woman at the Morgue.

"Moreover, my darling son," he concluded. "If you again sully your innocent young lips by speaking so much as one word to the animal I shall be forced to wash out your mouth with lye and scour you with a wire brush and Bordeaux Mixture."

Mrs. Appleton had merely dismissed Mr. Snarple as an impossible little creature, but pointed out that there were several perfectly good acres on which Squirt could carry on his activities and that there was no reason for his ever going anywhere near the Snarple property. All of which was probably why the east corner of the south field always seemed the most inviting spot to Robin Hood and his Merry Men.

The four veteran arrows had all scored near misses. Excalibur was fitted to the string and Squirt, muttering, "Now watch this, Friar," let go. It was practically a hit. The arrow did touch the willow wand, just enough to give it a slight wabble. And the wabble was just enough to make it strike a tuft of grass a glancing blow and, as arrows often will do, soar into the air with renewed vigor. And that renewed vigor carried it in a graceful arc high over the wall and landed it in the exact center of Mr. Snarple's garden.

With a sinking heart Arthur Amory cautiously reconnoitered. He stuck his head up over the wall just in time to meet Mr. Snarple's outraged glare, for of course Mr. Snarple *would* have picked just that moment to be in his garden and to be in such a spot that Excalibur had struck dangerously close to him.

"Aow, so there you are, you young pup," he snarled, and went on for some time in similar vein.

Squirt waited politely until there was a pause and then said, "I'm very sorry, Mr. Snarple, but it was a pure accident. The arrow just sort of ricocheted."

"Oh yes, and it might have just rickoshayed and just killed me."

"It wouldn't have killed you," said Squirt, starting to climb the wall, "and I'm very sorry but I'll *have* to get it. It's a very special arrow that my uncle brought me. It cost four dollars — plus tax."

"Four dollars hey, well there's four dollars you and your silly uncle can just kiss good-by to," yelped Mr. Snarple, starting for it.

Squirt continued to climb over the wall, then they both suddenly stopped, transfixed, for Excalibur, apparently of its own volition, was settling into the ground. With slow, even movements it sank down as though pulled by an invisible hand. Mr. Snarple leaped just as the bright orange cock feather disappeared beneath the surface. He grasped nothing, then his right foot plunged into the earth, up to the knee.

His momentum gave the knee a bad twist and for a short time he was trapped, his leg wedged into the hole. He bellowed horrifying threats and vituperation. Squirt decided that it was time for a strategic retreat; after all Excalibur was gone, there was no use lingering.

Sad and puzzled he gathered up the four old arrows and went over to where he had left his bow. As he leaned down to pick it up there was a slight commotion in the ground and General de Gaulle thrust his head and shoulders out into the sunshine. He grinned broadly and then drew back into the run. Squirt waited for his return, listening to the slowly subsiding racket in the Snarple garden. Suddenly he was astonished to see the shining steel point of an arrow emerging from the hole. Slowly it came into view, the clear polished shaft, the red, blue and gold stripes, finally the glowing orange cock feather. It was Excalibur, borne carefully in the mouth of the faithful General!

Arthur Amory leaped upon them both with wild cries of delight. Except for a little earth clinging to the feathers, which was easily brushed away, Excalibur was absolutely unharmed. De Gaulle, highly pleased with himself, received Squirt's praise and caresses with happy wrigglings.

Squirt could not resist racing down to the wall and peering into the garden. Mr. Snarple, limping slightly, was making his noisy way toward his house. At the garden gate he turned to direct a final glare in the direction of the Appleton property and beheld Squirt, triumphantly waving Excalibur with its unmistakable orange feather.

"Never mind, Mr. Snarple," Squirt called. "I've found it. I won't have to bother you."

As they went triumphantly up the hill, de Gaulle frisking joyously about his feet, Squirt looked back and could see the astonished countenance of Mr. Snarple glaring over the wall. His mouth was wide open, but no sound was coming from it.

Under the circumstances Squirt decided that it was wisest not to mention the incident at home, but he did write in the Book of Tricks:

#39. *The best one of all. To rescue arrows by the Underground Method. This is a $4 Trick — plus tax.*

Although not mentioned, the incident did become known in the home almost immediately, in a rather unexpected fashion. An hour or so after Excalibur's rescue Pearlacy interrupted Mr. Appleton's work to announce a Mr. Snodgrass, Town Dog Warden.

Mr. Appleton, who had just completed a chapter which had come out quite well, received the cause of the interruption with less irritation than usual. In fact he was so pleased with the chapter that he was almost cordial.

The Dog Warden was a tall, lanky individual with a straggly

mustache and the most prominent and active Adam's apple that Mr. Appleton could ever remember having seen. The visitor accepted a chair and a cigarette with slight awkwardness, cleared his throat and made his errand known.

"I've got to find out about your, now, dog, Mr. Appleton," he said. "If you know what I mean."

"I am afraid I do not," Mr. Appleton answered.

"Well now I've had information that you've got a dog, but I didn't think you did have, so I looked up in the records at Town Hall and there ain't any dog registered in your name and no license issued. There's got to be a license if you've got a dog."

"For once," smiled Mr. Appleton, "the Town Hall records seem to be correct. There is no dog registered in our name and no license issued because we have no dog. We have not possessed a dog in some eight years. Mrs. Appleton, unfortunately, is allergic to dogs."

"My wife doesn't care for them either," Mr. Snodgrass confided. "Seems sort of funny with my business, you might say, being concerned with dogs, but she just doesn't like 'em and that's that. Some women are just that way, if you know what I mean."

"It is hay fever," Mr. Appleton explained, "dog fur gives her hay fever."

"You don't say," wondered the Warden. "Now ain't that something. My brother-in-law has it something terrible, hay fever I mean, but he hasn't got any dog. He always thought it was hay give it to him, if you know what I mean, so he sold his farm and took a factory job over in Bridgeport, but he has it worse than ever. Must be something else does it."

"About this supposed dog of ours?" Mr. Appleton prompted.

"Oh yes," said Mr. Snodgrass, "your dog. Now this party that gave the information is also making a complaint about damage to his garden. Says your dog dug a hole in his garden. He stepped in it and hurt his leg. I saw the hole but it don't look like any hole a dog dug, if you know what I mean. There's no dirt around it. Now when a dog digs a hole he tears up the whole place and makes a mess of dirt bigger than the hole.\ This hole's a clean round hole, no dirt around at all. I told him so and it was probably a drain or something just settled, if you know what I mean, but he swears you've got a dog, and the dog dug the hole and he wants the law on you."

A suspicion of the true facts of the matter began to dawn on Mr. Appleton and placed him in an awkward quandary. General de Gaulle was certainly not a dog; at the same time it would be a difficult and embarrassing task to persuade the Warden, or anyone else, that he was a mole. Moreover, Uncle Amory had insisted most firmly that no news of this phenomenal creature be allowed to leak out or any harm come to him. The situation was made more complicated by the fact, which he now noted, that Squirt and the General were at this moment engaged in playing the U-boat game in plain view of the window. He turned to his guest, saying hastily, "This wild goose chase, Mr. Snodgrass, has been a rather unnecessary bother to you. How about a drink?"

"Well now," cried the Warden heartily, "I certainly wouldn't have any aller — whatever it is your wife has about dogs — to that, if you know what I mean."

Mr. Appleton hastily mixed two highballs, strong ones, and offered one to the visitor. "This — party," he asked, "who has the grievance is — ?"

"Why this here Snardle or Snarple or whatever it is, lives next to you," said Mr. Snodgrass, sampling the highball approvingly. "Noisy little guy, if you know what I mean."

"I do indeed," agreed Mr. Appleton. From up the hill he could hear a series of heavy spade thumps, indicating exploding depth bombs. He talked rapidly and exhaustively while the Warden absorbed his highball. He discoursed on allergies, dogs, hay fever, the weather, children, literature, gardens and neighbors. He talked of the proposed new highway, the past election and the coming election and unobtrusively let it be known that he himself had always voted for the party under which Mr. Snodgrass held office, and always expected to.

Eventually the Warden finished his drink, wrung out his mustache and prepared to depart. "Thanks, Mr. Appleton," he said. "That just hit the spot, if you know what I mean." He

64

stepped to the window and looked out approvingly. "Nice place you've got here. Haven't been up here sence old John McCormick used to raise onions on this field."

Suddenly his eye lighted on Squirt, around whose feet General de Gaulle was gaily capering. A strained silence fell. The Warden's Adam's apple bounced up and down like a buoy in a choppy channel. "Sa-a-a-y — " he began.

At this moment the Nazi U-boat upended itself and disappeared smoothly into the ground. Mr. Snodgrass turned a reproachful eye on his host, on his empty glass and then back at

the landscape where Squirt was now dashing about striking heavy blows with the spade. "What was that I seen?" he demanded accusingly.

"*That?*" said Mr. Appleton, looking out. "Why, that's my son, Arthur Amory, great boy, you'll have to meet him. I'll call him down."

"I mean that other thing," the Warden persisted. "I'd swear I saw something. It went into the ground — "

"Come, come, old man," laughed Mr. Appleton, clapping him on the shoulder, "your eyes must be playing tricks on you. I don't see a thing and I can assure you positively there is no dog. There hasn't been a dog here in eight years."

Mr. Snodgrass shook his head sharply, rubbed his eyes and took one more long look, while his Adam's apple gradually resumed its normal rise and fall. "Guess it was just one of them allergees," he finally said. "If you know what I mean."

Mr. Appleton saw him to his car and bade him a pleasant farewell, then strode up the hill. The U-boat had just surfaced and was wallowing helplessly in a heavy sea.

"My darling son," said Mr. Appleton. "You will kindly bed down your little playmate and then report to me in the study. I feel that there are some explanations due, IF you know what I mean."

Chapter 6

MAN WITH A HOE

IN THE INTERVIEW with his father Squirt was thoroughly impressed with the necessity of keeping General de Gaulle's existence from becoming common knowledge. He therefore taught the General Interesting Trick #40, *To Take Refuge Underground at the Approach of Danger.*

It was fortunate that he did, for a state of undeclared war now existed with Mr. Snarple. The very next morning, evidently at the request of the enemy, a State Policeman arrived in his car. Mr. Appleton found him less easy to deal with than the Dog Warden, for he refused any refreshment and showed no interest in conversation, but stamped around the grounds in a most important manner, searching for an unlicensed dog or other destructive animal.

Since Mr. Appleton's chapter for that day was not going too well and as the Policeman managed to twist his ankle badly in one of de Gaulle's holes, the whole affair became quite unpleasant. The sight of the police car and the uniform also had a shat-

tering effect on Pearlacy's morale and made lunch late and quite inedible, which did not add to the general happiness. General de Gaulle, however, had learned Trick #40 well and stayed below until the skies had cleared, so no great harm was done.

The shock to Pearlacy's nerves strengthened her dislike of Mr. Snarple and made her a firm and active ally of Squirt and the General. The location of the kitchen gave her an excellent vantage point for observing and reporting on the activities of Mr. Snarple.

"He's got a old pair of opry glasses or something," she warned Squirt, "and he keeps a peeking over the wall thu 'em. You and the Ginral better keep away from that field down there."

They did keep away from it, but evidently Mr. Snarple must have caught some glimpses of the General, for there was another visit from the State Officer and two more from the Dog Warden during the week. Pearlacy kept a sharp eye on the driveway and always heralded the arrival of these visitors by a loud whoop which the General soon learned to recognize as the signal for Trick #40. Before the arriving cars had come to a stop he was always well below the surface.

The Dog Warden really seemed more interested in Mr. Appleton's conversation — and highballs — than in locating any elusive dog. After the third visit Mr. Appleton began to be a bit bored by these interruptions and somewhat out of patience with the General as the cause of them.

"It isn't fair to be cross with de Gaulle," Mrs. Appleton protested. "It certainly is not his fault; it's all that nosey little Snarple creature's doing. And if you would stop giving that Dog Warden so many highballs I'm sure he wouldn't come so often or stay so long."

"Mr. Snodgrass is a charming person," her husband replied. "He has a most expressive Adam's apple and is a thoroughly appreciative listener — if you know what I mean."

"I am afraid you will have to spade up the beds in the upper garden for me," she said. "James has the grippe and will not be able to come this week and I simply *must* get my annuals in."

"My dear," said Mr. Appleton hastily, "that is quite impossible. I am in the midst of a most important chapter. I cannot possibly spare the time and moreover it makes my back ache. The very thought of it makes my back ache."

"Nonsense," she replied. "You have plenty of time to spend talking to that Snodgrass person. It will do you good. Dr. Morgan says you need exercise, and it won't take you long."

"It will not take me long; it will not take me any time at all, for I have not the slightest intention of becoming a muzhik at my time of life. I am not the peasant type. I am — "

"The plants are coming at noon tomorrow," Mrs. Appleton went on, "so you will have to do it right after breakfast. Spread some lime on it first and be sure you rake it well."

"Why can't Squirt do it?" he protested sulkily.

"— And get all the stones out. You know it is entirely too heavy for Amie. I will put out your gardening shoes tonight and your old trousers. I think it is going to be a lovely day."

"Your idea of a lovely day and my idea of a lovely day are much, much farther apart than the North and South Poles," Mr. Appleton said. "The difference could be more aptly compared to that between the earth and Mars, or perhaps Saturn."

"— And don't forget about the lime," Mrs. Appleton reminded him.

In the morning Mr. Appleton grumbled and fussed as temperamentally as an Arctic explorer outfitting himself for an expedition. Two different pairs of shoes were tried and discarded and a third complained of as uncomfortable. Choosing the proper shirt took half an hour, a certain hat had to be found, then a pair of canvas gloves. At nine-thirty there was a news broadcast which must be listened to, then there were several long-distance telephone calls to make, all imperative.

"Goodness," Pearlacy confided to Squirt, "your pa certainly do take on over digging up a couple of little old beds. James would have had 'em dug and planted before breakfast and swep the garage too."

What with one thing and another it was well along toward eleven before Mr. Appleton reluctantly approached his appointed task. He found Squirt and General de Gaulle frisking about the garden and regarded them with a sour eye.

"Father, I've spread all the lime," Squirt cried, "and I've brought the baskets for the stones and the rake and the wheelbarrow and I've taught the General a new trick, a very interesting one."

"Where is the spading fork?" demanded his father.

"I don't know. It isn't in the tool house. I think Mother loaned it to Mrs. Carstairs, but I'm not sure. But you must see de Gaulle's new trick."

"If there is anything in the world I do not wish to see, it is a new trick," Mr. Appleton said. "You will kindly take yourself and your lumbering pet to some far distant spot. I do not wish you to witness your father's shame. To think that at my age I have been driven to tilling the soil — "

"This is Trick #41," Squirt explained, "and it's a very interesting one."

"One more mention of tricks," said Mr. Appleton, seating himself on the wheelbarrow and filling his pipe, "or one more repetition of the words 'very interesting' and I shall take you and your oversized friend by the napes of your respective necks and drop you into Mr. Snarple's garden, with a cordial invitation to him to do his worst."

While he was speaking Squirt and the General had placed themselves at one corner of the largest bed. The General set himself like a sprinter at the mark.

"Look, Father," Squirt called. "Here is Trick #41."

He clapped his hands sharply and de Gaulle plunged beneath the surface. Down the length of the bed he progressed, just beneath the surface, stirring up the earth like a rotary plow, at an astonishing speed. As he reached the far end Squirt stamped twice and de Gaulle reversed himself as sharply as a racing swimmer in an indoor pool and came back in a straight parallel run. Another double stamp as he reached the near end and the process was repeated.

"You see, Father," Squirt explained, "all we'll have to do now is to rake it and gather up the stones."

Mr. Appleton relaxed and lighted his pipe. "I see, I see," he smiled happily. "#41 is indeed a splendid accomplishment. I feel, my son, that you must have inherited a slight portion of your father's mental brilliance. I am also delighted to note your use of the word 'we' in connection with the matter of raking and gathering up the stones. Suppose you take the rake and begin it, while I assume this important task of stamping."

73

Squirt raked, Mr. Appleton smoked his pipe and occasionally stamped. The sun shone, the birds sang and General de Gaulle churned back and forth steadily. In almost no time the largest bed was done, the General drank two bowls of water and whisked through the two smaller beds at top speed.

Mr. Appleton did help in gathering up the stones and carrying them up to the trash heap, and well before noon the flower beds lay smoothly raked, soft and inviting. General de Gaulle, slightly blown, but very proud of himself, stretched in the sunshine.

After lunch Mr. Appleton drove down to the village. When he returned he found his wife, Squirt and the General busily engaged in setting out small plants. Here again, de Gaulle was proving a great aid. Preceding Mrs. Appleton down the rows he scooped out neat, evenly spaced holes with his trowel-like forepaws. Mrs. Appleton set the plants and Squirt carried the water.

"A charming picture of communal effort," Mr. Appleton remarked, seating himself on the wheelbarrow. "A splendidly efficient system, made quite perfect by the fact that there seems no place in it reserved for me."

"Oh, Arthur," his wife cried happily, straightening up and pushing a bit of hair out of her eyes, "you did a perfectly mar-

velous job of digging the beds. James has never prepared them as beautifully as this."

"A mere nothing," he answered pleasantly. "When an Appleton does a thing he does it thoroughly, an old family trait, which I hope our son will inherit. By the way, son, when you have finished your little tasks here you will find in the rear seat of the car a package containing one dozen new arrows. Unfortunately our local shops do not offer anything as pretentious as your uncle's gift, but these are the very best seventy-five centers and should serve for everyday use. I only wish there were some worthy token of esteem, something in gold or platinum, that I could procure for your little playmate. I did, however, get him a fresh box of Bities; your original supply must be slightly stale by now, and de Gaulle deserves only the best."

"Dr. Morgan was certainly right about your needing exercise," Mrs. Appleton said, straightening up again. "That little digging seems to have done your spirits and disposition a world of good. The only thing I can't quite understand is how you managed it without the spading fork. I loaned it to Alice Carstairs last week and forgot all about it. She just brought it back this afternoon."

"Oh, *that?*" Mr. Appleton said lightly, looking very hard at Squirt. "That is a secret of the Appleton men, is it not, my son?"

"Yes indeed, Father, and thank you ever so much for the arrows. I think I will call them the Twelve Apostles."

Uncle Amory was coming that evening for the week end. In the late afternoon, before going to the train to meet him, Squirt, aided by Pearlacy, managed to open the new box of Bities.

"Father bought General St. Lucien Beauregard a fresh box of Bities," Squirt explained. "He thought maybe the old ones were getting a little stale."

"They certainly look stale," she agreed, peering in the old box. "Gray like and sort of mildewed. Don't smell very good either. I'll chuck 'em out later."

Uncle Amory descended from the train bubbling with energy and good spirits. He was bearing a slender package which was thrust at Squirt with a jovial, "Well, well, well, splendid, splendid. Something for you, Squirt, something for you. Another arrow; same kind, same outrageous price, same idiotic clerk. Hope you'll like it, hope you'll like it. How's the General?"

"He's just fine, Amory," Mrs. Appleton answered, "and growing at the same rate, or a little faster. And at last I think we can have our bridge game. Alice Carstairs is coming over after dinner to make a fourth."

"Fine, fine," he beamed. "Miserable player, miserable player. Hope her game's improved."

"The pot hoping the kettle is *less* black," Mr. Appleton muttered, starting up with a back-snapping jerk.

"Arthur, *do* be more careful," Mrs. Appleton protested. "And I think the brake is still on."

"It is," Squirt said. "Father *always* leaves the brake on. I am going to call this new arrow Daniel Boone, Uncle Amory. I have a very interesting lot of arrows now; Excalibur, Daniel Boone, the Twelve Apostles and the Four Horsemen; those are the four old ones. And we're going to have chocolate soufflé for dinner."

On the drive home Uncle Amory informed them that his Paper was progressing splendidly and that the photographs had all come out well. "By George, it's going to create a sensation," he bubbled, "a positive sensation. Never been anything like it, never. I'll read some of it to you this evening. Like to have your opinion."

"Bridge, I believe, has been planned for this evening, but I'm sure we'd all much rather hear your paper," Mr. Appleton began hopefully.

"Oh, yes, of course, of course. Forgot bridge," Uncle Amory said. "Plenty of time for the Paper tomorrow. No, no. Bridge by all means. Mustn't disappoint the ladies, eh, Helen?"

Helen's expression did not indicate any great fear of disappointment one way or the other.

At home Uncle Amory could scarcely wait to see de Gaulle. The General recognized him and at once did the special trick of standing on his head, while Uncle Amory scrambled in his bag for tapes, rules, calipers, scales and notebooks. It was soon determined that in the two weeks since the last visit General de Gaulle had grown seven inches in length, a corresponding amount in girth and had added sixty-seven ounces to his weight. He was now about as large as a medium-sized seal.

"Amazing, amazing," Uncle Amory cried, jotting down his notes. "More and more preposterous, perfectly impossible, quite ridiculous — yet it is *true* and authenticated. Arthur, will you sign these notes as witness; you too, Helen? Ought to have a third — how about Pearlacy?"

"At the moment Pearlacy is frantically engaged with a chocolate soufflé," Mrs. Appleton said. "She is also completely undone with excitement over the photograph of herself that you brought, and besides, she can't write."

"I'll sign it," Squirt volunteered.

"You are a minor," his father pointed out. "In fact, if you will pardon a poor pun, you bear all the earmarks of a coal miner. Go and try to get yourself clean before dinner. At least try to remove the more obvious layers."

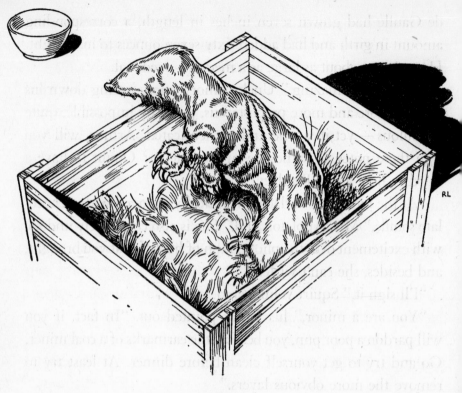

Chapter 7

FOOD CRISIS

IT WAS QUITE LATE before the bridge game got under way. Uncle Amory had brought a great sheaf of photographs of de Gaulle, the result of Mr. Fulton's busy day, and these all had to be examined and commented on. Mr. Appleton's examinations and comments were long and leisurely, with frequent hopeful glances at the clock. When Mrs. Carstairs arrived he insisted that she see each and every picture, so it was well past nine-thirty when the table was finally set up.

Cards had been shuffled and dealt. Uncle Amory, for the third time, had started to explain his new bidding system when Squirt, pajama clad and wide eyed with distress, burst into the living room.

"Mother," he wailed, "de Gaulle is sick. There's something the matter with him. He didn't eat any supper; he wouldn't touch the new Bities. He's acting awfully queer and I'm afraid he's going to suc- suc- cumb!" The thought opened the floodgates and he flung himself on Mrs. Appleton, upsetting the table and scattering a shower of cards, glasses and ash trays on the rug, on Mrs. Carstairs and Uncle Amory.

The game was forgotten as they all trooped up to Squirt's room. De Gaulle was in his bed, now enlarged to a sizable packing box, and was obviously a very sick General. His round solid body seemed to have suddenly lost its bulk and hung pitifully from his frame. At the sound of visitors he tried to sit up and smile, his tail stirred feebly. Squirt burst into fresh roars of anguish.

"Shall I call up the vet?" Mrs. Carstairs began, "Dr. Fillow is —"

Uncle Amory turned an outraged glare on her and Mrs. Appleton whispered hastily, "Amory is one of the most famous

81

naturalists in the world, Alice; he'll know what to do."

Uncle Amory took charge, throwing his coat on the bed and snapping orders like a fire chief at a conflagration.

"Squirt," he cried, "that little black bag on my bureau. Arthur, get something warm, sweaters or something. Helen, a heating pad and a flashlight and hot water." He glanced indignantly at Mrs. Carstairs. "You," he said, "might go down and pick up the cards and ash trays. Vet indeed! Preposterous!"

He had de Gaulle's paw now and was taking his pulse, frowning worriedly. Squirt returned with the bag and his uncle snatched out a stethoscope and listened carefully to various parts of de Gaulle's anatomy. He took his blood pressure, looked down his throat and examined the narrow tongue. He felt and poked him all over, took his temperature, wrapped him in Mr. Appleton's best sweater and applied the heating pad.

"Weakness," he finally pronounced. "Obvious lack of nourishment. Squirt, what was this you were saying about changing his diet?"

Arthur Amory stifled his sobs enough to explain, "Father brought him a fresh box of Bities; he thought the old ones were stale. I gave him some of these new ones for supper, but he wouldn't touch them. He seemed to be hungry because he sat up and opened his mouth and b- b- begged." The memory brought a new outburst of roars.

"Ridiculous," snapped Uncle Amory. "Shouldn't have done

82

it, shouldn't have done it. Slight difference in taste doubtless, animals temperamental that way. Where are the old ones? Try those."

"Pearlacy said she was going to throw them out."

Pearlacy, attracted by Squirt's bellowings and the general confusion, had now appeared, clad in a magenta dressing gown of quilted rayon, her eyes gleaming like ping-pong balls.

"I thowed 'em out this evening, in the trash barl or the garbage can, I don't recollect which. One was full and I thown 'em in the other, but I'm too confused to remember which was the full one. Poor Ginral," she cried, kneeling beside the bed. "He's hongry and I don thowed out his Bities." De Gaulle stirred weakly, opening his mouth and Pearlacy added her tears to Squirt's.

"Come, Arthur," Uncle Amory ordered. "We must find them at once. The *Talpidae* go very quickly if deprived of food too long."

"It's raining cats and dogs," Mrs. Carstairs contributed helpfully.

There was a general rush for rubbers and raincoats. Squirt donned oilskins and a sou'wester. Mr. Appleton found his rubber coat and an old hat, but the only thing available for Uncle Amory was Mrs. Appleton's best raincoat. It was a beautiful creation of white silk with rows of shiny chromium buttons, extremely swagger on Mrs. Appleton, but quite the opposite on

Uncle Amory. As it was cut in quite sharply at the waist and as Uncle Amory cut out quite sharply at the waist there was some trouble in keeping it closed, which was solved by Mrs. Carstairs tying a brilliant pink scarf around his middle.

It was raining more than cats and dogs outside. It was raining sheets, streams and little fishes. Moreover there was a howling northeast wind which blew the rain horizontally and up, as well as down. The turnaround was a shallow lake and the spot behind the garage where the trash resided was ankle deep in mud and water. A clogged roof gutter was sending down a miniature Niagara.

Squirt plunged frantically at the garbage can, hurling out its contents like an eager fox terrier. Mr. Appleton held the flashlight while Uncle Amory tried unsuccessfully to keep Mrs. Appleton's raincoat closed, hold up an umbrella and dodge the flying garbage. Then Mr. Appleton dropped the flashlight in the mud, Uncle Amory stepped on it and the search was brought to a temporary halt.

"Arthur," called Mrs. Appleton from the kitchen door. "Why don't you take them in the garage where you can see?"

"There happen to be two cars in the garage," he roared.

"Well, you *could* move one of them out," she answered, not unreasonably. "And don't shout so."

So after a few false starts Mr. Appleton managed to back the station wagon out and into the retaining wall, thoroughly smashing one rear fender and the taillight. With much heaving, slithering and splashing the garbage can and trash barrel were dragged into the garage. The shelter and light did make the search easier, but the closeness of the garage and the steamy atmosphere did not make it an appetizing one.

Squirt, blubbering and panting, scattered the noisome contents of the can about the floor and on Uncle Amory with renewed vigor, but no success in the way of Bities.

"I wish someone could explain just why garbage always seems to consist of ninety-five per cent coffee grounds and orange skins," Mr. Appleton growled.

"There seem to be plenty of other things," said Uncle Amory, disgustedly wiping his hands on Mrs. Carstairs' scarf, "every sort of loathsome item — but Bities. Here, Arthur, help me dump this trash barrel and see what luck we have there."

Together he and Mr. Appleton upended the barrel and Squirt plunged at the heap of trash. His efforts were at length rewarded, for at the very bottom of the pile the brightly colored Bities package finally came to light. Most of its contents had been spilled and were hopelessly mixed with the gleanings of carpet sweeper, vacuum cleaner and scrap baskets, but an inch or so of the gray, mouldy-looking flakes still remained in the bottom of the box.

"Fine, fine, splendid, splendid," shouted Uncle Amory. He stepped on an empty toothpowder can, executed an ungraceful pirouette and fell heavily in the mess.

Squirt did not wait to aid. With a glad cry he raced into the kitchen and upstairs, leaving a scattered trail of mud, water, garbage and assorted odors. Without removing his streaming oil-skins he knelt down by the sickbed and with trembling hands poured out a few of the hard won Bities.

The General weakly raised his head and stuck out a feeble tongue. As he dimly recognized the aroma of his beloved food the tongue snapped rapidly and took in three whole flakes. A quiver passed through his emaciated body, he staggered to his feet and eagerly lapped up a bowl of water. Gratefully he licked Squirt's fingers, twitched a few times, curled up in Mr. Appleton's sweater and went to sleep. Already, to Squirt's tear-blurred eyes, the General's form seemed to be assuming its old round-ness, his fur its soft, rich sheen.

"You Mr. Squirt, take off them wet close and get into the bath tub," said Pearlacy from the doorway. "I've drawed you a big, deep tub of good hot water, with some mustard in it. Get into it quick now. I'll watch the Ginral."

Mr. Appleton staggered into the kitchen assisting Uncle Amory, whose appearance sent Mrs. Carstairs fleeing in helpless hysterics. The beautiful once-white raincoat was dripping water and garbage. The fall into the trash pile had further decorated it with tufts of dust, lint, ashes and cigarette butts. The pink scarf had run, copiously and spectacularly.

"Get those wet things off now," Mrs. Appleton ordered,

struggling with her own laughter. "Alice and I have made you some nice hot coffee."

"COFFEE?" roared Uncle Amory, wiping a large smear of grounds from his left cheek. "I never want to see, *or* smell the horrible stuff as long as I live — or oranges. I want a hot toddy, very hot and *very* strong and very soon."

Later, Mrs. Appleton drew her husband aside to say, "I'm sorry Arthur, but you'll have to drive Alice home. I hate to ask you to, but Amory has the guest room."

"Not at all, not at all, my dear," Mr. Appleton smiled genially. "I shall be forced to use your car, for the station wagon seems to be slightly crippled, but all has worked out for the best. Do you realize that once again, due to the providential presence of the General, we have escaped your brother's peculiar version of bridge? Good old de Gaulle!"

In the morning General de Gaulle was flourishing; fat, frisky and amiable as of old. He had eaten three flakes of the salvaged Bities for breakfast and washed them down with two large bowls of water.

Uncle Amory, however, was not especially festive. He felt a cold coming on and sneezed frequently to prove it. He managed, though, to overcome his distaste of coffee and oranges enough to enjoy a hearty breakfast, after which he became deeply engrossed in the question of de Gaulle's diet.

He spread out samples of the old and new Bities and examined them with great thoroughness. He looked at them through a magnifying glass, he crumbled them to compare their texture, he smelled them and even tasted them.

"Preposterous," he finally announced. "Ridiculous, absurd. These are not the same thing at all. Completely different in smell, taste and texture. Have to have them analyzed to find what the difference is, but there certainly is a difference, a vast difference. This may be the explanation of this strange growth of de Gaulle. Difference in taste is especially noticeable. The new ones have no taste at all, but these old ones have a nasty, sulphurous, musty flavor." He moistened his finger, picked up a few flakes and tasted them with a wry look. "Here, Arthur, you try."

"Thank you, NO," said Mr. Appleton firmly. "I once tasted some, passing through the outskirts of Lorain, Ohio. I have no intention of repeating either ordeal again."

Uncle Amory filled a small bottle with the old, original Bities and another with the new ones, labelled them carefully and packed them in his bag.

"I will have an analysis made as soon as I get back to town tomorrow," he promised. "There is something distinctly peculiar about this, distinctly peculiar. Now I think I shall take a nap. Helen, may I trouble you for an aspirin and a little soda. I am *sure* I am taking a cold. It's still raining, isn't it?"

"In sheets," Mr. Appleton said. "For myself, I shall read the Sunday papers while our stalwart little son cleans up that horrid mess in the garage. De Gaulle may do whatever he pleases."

Uncle Amory did not reappear until suppertime. He was much

refreshed by the long rest and the cold was temporarily subdued, but there seemed to be considerable difficulty about his coat and collar.

"Confounded clothes seem to have shrunk," he complained. "Must have gotten wetter than I realized last night. Helen, did Pearlacy do anything to this suit?"

"Not a thing," Mrs. Appleton answered, gazing wonderingly at him. "Just hung it up; it was barely damp." She paused and suddenly said, "Amory, stand up a moment and let me look at you."

He did, protestingly, and Mr. Appleton snickered.

"Amory," he said, "go over to the door. Squirt, get the yard-stick. Now," he continued, when his brother-in-law, still pro-testing, had straightened himself against the measuring post, "do you know your former exact height?"

"Former, *former?*" Uncle Amory sputtered. "Ridiculous, absurd. Height's exactly five feet, three and a quarter. Hasn't changed a fraction in the past twenty years." Mr. Appleton, hum-ming pleasantly, marked the height with a book, then measured carefully with the yardstick.

"Your height, my dear relative," he announced, "may not have varied a fraction in the past twenty years, but it *has* in-creased exactly one and three-quarters inches since this morning, when you were idiotic enough to taste those Bities. I remarked some time ago that there was something definitely screwy about them."

"Preposterous," shouted Uncle Amory. "Impossible. You are not funny, Arthur. Not at all funny."

He snatched the yardstick and did his own measuring. He made Mrs. Appleton use the book and Squirt verify it. He measured it again, still the answer came out the same — five feet five.

He unbuttoned his collar, which was now far too tight, sat down and stirred his coffee in a deep study.

"General de Gaulle had two extra flakes today," he finally said. "Let's see if that has made any difference."

They waked the sleeping General and made careful measurements. Surely enough, de Gaulle's growth for the day was three-quarters of an inch, instead of the usual half inch.

"As you say, Arthur," Uncle Amory admitted. "There is something screwy about this, distinctly screwy."

Chapter 8

AND THE FLOODS CAME

ON MONDAY it was still raining. At lunch time there came
a telegram from Uncle Amory which read:

MOST IMPERATIVE SQUIRT RESCUE EVERY POSSIBLE FLAKE OLD
ORIGINAL BITIES HIGHLY IMPORTANT STOP AM WRITING DETAILS.

"Sixteen words," said Mrs. Appleton, counting them up on her
fingers, "it *must* be important. Well, Amie, I'm afraid you will

have to spend the afternoon clawing over that trash again. Never mind, de Gaulle will help you and it's too wet to do anything else anyway."

De Gaulle did help, most efficiently. Squirt again spread out the contents of the trash barrel which he had so dutifully cleaned up the previous day, then together they carefully went through all the litter. The General's sharp nose located many flakes which otherwise might have been missed. With his broad fore-paws he turned over the trash with great speed and interest and by mid afternoon they had salvaged a good double handful of the precious provender.

Their labors were interrupted by the arrival of Mr. Swain's garbage truck which roared up the driveway in a welter of flying mud and water. Its sudden approach trapped de Gaulle in the garage. Trick #40 was out of the question, but the General smartly ran over to a dim corner where some fertilizer bags stood, turned his back, hunched himself up and remained immovable, looking exactly like a bag of bone meal.

"Hiya, Sitting Bull?" Mr. Swain greeted, stepping in out of the weather and eyeing the disorder. "What's going on, lose something?"

"Big Chief hunt for valuable treasure," Squirt replied in his best pidgin Choctaw. "Big Chief find um bimeby."

"Silver likely," Enoch went on. "People's always throwing silver out. Two ladies were over to the dump most of last Friday with their shoffer, poking around after a couple of teaspoons the cook thought she'd throwed out. They found plenty of stuff all right, but wasn't any of it silver, not by a long shot. Stirred up a bunch of rats after a while and then they quit. Ever see any of them rats over to the dump? Big as tomcats, some of 'em — mean too.

"What was it, teaspoons or butter spreaders? Those butter spreaders are always getting throwed out, I've got a whole dozen I've collected. Don't many of them match, but they're all solid silver. I gave them to the wife for Christmas but she didn't have any use for 'em so she gave 'em to her niece for a wedding present. *She's* real proud of 'em. Uses 'em too, sometimes."

Squirt did not care to reveal the object of his search, so he confined his reply to several "Ugh's" and the reassurance that, "Big Chief findum, bimeby."

"Well, good picking," called Enoch, climbing back into the Deadwood Coach. "I'll be back Thursday." He reached behind

the seat and tossed the missing arrow into the garage chuckling, "Here's something else I found — darned near made a bull's-eye."

"Oh, thank you very much," Squirt cried. "Big Chief very grateful to paleface. Big Chief will ambush stage Thursday — if it ever stops raining."

"Ain't this rain something?" agreed Mr. Swain. "Well, take it easy Chief." He backed around and splashed off down the drive.

"That was very smart of you, General," Squirt said, as de Gaulle relaxed and capered back to his task. "I will put that down as Interesting Trick #42. *To Imitate a bag of Bone Meal.*"

The rain was indeed something. All afternoon while Squirt and de Gaulle cleaned up the mess, refilled the trash barrel and swept the garage floor the rain continued to drum steadily on the roof.

At dinner Pearlacy announced gloomily, "The cellar's flooding."

"Oh dear," Mrs. Appleton said. "We really should have had a drain put in, Arthur. Every time we have a bad rain the cellar gets flooded."

"Of course we really should have," Mr. Appleton snorted. "There are at least fourteen other things we really should have done and have not. This particular little operation would now mean tearing up the entire front lawn and making an excavation in the family exchequer that would leave it a hollow shell. Besides, you can't hire anyone to dig anything nowadays anyway."

"What are you going to do?" she asked.

"Do? I shall do what I always do when the cellar gets flooded. First I shall call our useless plumber and be told that his flooded-cellar-expert is on a vacation and that their cellar pump is engaged for the next ten days. Then I shall don arctics, which by the way leak, and assisted by our stalwart son, will spend a sloppy evening in the cellar lifting heavy, useless things off the floor and putting them on higher places. If the water rises high enough to endanger the life of the oil burner we will remove that and place it out of harm's way. Otherwise there will be no hot water the rest of the summer and probably no hot steam next winter — "

"It's almost up to it now," Pearlacy volunteered. "It's coming in awful fast, you can hear it running if you lissen."

"Thank you, I do not care to listen," Mr. Appleton said. "My back is beginning to ache already and I can think of some forty thousand sounds to which I would rather listen. One of them is the cheery clink of coffee cups in the living room."

After coffee he and Squirt donned their wading gear and descended to the cellar. Pearlacy had not exaggerated — it *was* coming in awful fast. You could hear it and also see it; squirting in from the rear wall in thin, crystal-clear sprays, in driblets and in large clay-colored spouts. The flood was even now lapping about the legs of the oil burner. Scraps of paper and chips of kindling floated on the surface.

They spent a busy half hour moving boxes of books, stacks of magazines and various other heavy things to higher and drier locations, while Mrs. Appleton and Pearlacy offered occasional advice and encouragement from the stairs. Mr. Appleton's arctics did leak, also Squirt managed to drop a box of books which thoroughly splashed them both and did not add to the feeling of good fellowship and co-operation. By now the water had risen halfway up the legs of the oil burner and Mr. Appleton regarded it with a sour eye as he sighed wearily.

"If you could possibly manage to bring pliers, assorted wrenches and the other necessary tools without dropping more than two-thirds of them," he said to his son, "we had best begin the horrid and back-breaking task of rescuing the burner. Not that I particularly care for the filthy thing, but your mother and Pearlacy are both afflicted with an incurable weakness for hot water, a failing which has certainly not been inherited by our only son and heir."

But Squirt was not listening — that is to Mr. Appleton. He was bending down at the far side of the cellar, his ear pressed against the wet, dripping wall. He held up a hand and called excitedly, "Wait a minute, be quiet everybody. I hear something."

For a moment there was no sound save for the steady gurgle and splash of the incoming streams. Then suddenly they could all hear a distinct scratching sound against the wall, just below Squirt's ear. Wildly he pounded with his fist and the scratching became more violent. One cement block in the lowest course moved slightly, the mortar crumbled around its edges.

Splashing recklessly, Squirt rushed to the other room and came back with a hatchet. He struck two or three sharp blows on the loose block and pried energetically at the joints. Before their astonished eyes the almost submerged block wobbled slightly, then slowly slid outward.

The water started out with a rush, but was temporarily blocked

as the sleek head and stout body of General de Gaulle wedged
itself in through the opening. For a moment it looked as though
he were going to stick; he gasped for air and scrambled frantically. Squirt grasped the broad forepaws, braced his foot against
the wall and pulled hard. Slowly, with the sucking sound of a

gigantic cork being drawn, the General was pulled in through the hole. As the suction was released Squirt toppled backward into the water, his rescued companion sprawling on his chest.

Eddying and gurgling the imprisoned flood swirled out, so rapidly that by the time Squirt and de Gaulle had righted themselves and taken refuge on the steps large patches of floor were beginning to show here and there, like the reappearing earth after the Deluge.

Mr. Appleton, somewhat dazed, bowed deeply in the general direction of his wife. "Madame desired a drain, I believe," he said. "Madame *has* a drain, a magnificent drain!" He went over and peered into the hole, down which a few trickles were still running. "Probably the most magnificent drain this side of the Croton Aqueduct."

Pearlacy fetched a large bath towel and the General was given a thorough rubdown, while Squirt was sent up for a hot bath. Although the evening was warm Mr. Appleton built a brisk log fire in the living room. While he dried his wet feet de Gaulle basked happily in the warm firelight and in the admiration of the household.

Squirt, scrubbed, dried and wrapped in a dressing gown, came down to collect his pal. Pearlacy appeared to announce that the rain had ceased.

"It would," Mr. Appleton said. "It always stops the moment all difficulties have been overcome. Now that we have a drain it

will probably never rain again."

"I wondered what he wanted to go out for," Pearlacy said. "Right after dinner he come down to the kitchen and wanted to go out, so I let him. He certainly is a smart Ginral, ain't you St. Lucien Beauregard?"

"He certainly is," Squirt agreed proudly. He produced the Book of Interesting Tricks and read: "#43. *To Construct Drains.*"

"May I suggest that you insert the adjective *magnificent?*" Mr. Appleton said. "*Magnificent drains* would sound far better."

So Squirt added *magniffisent.*

Next morning, as though to atone for its ill behavior of the past few days, the weather was gorgeous. The sky was blue, fresh washed leaves and grass were glistening brilliant green, the gentle breeze was warm and balmy.

In the station wagon Mr. Appleton and his son rolled peacefully down the driveway, village-bound for cigarettes — and perhaps a few arrows.

Suddenly Squirt started as though stung. "Goodness gracious," he gasped. "*Look* at Mr. Snarple's garden!"

His father looked, jammed on the brakes and the car slithered to a stop. "Goodness gracious, and a couple of Mercy Me's," Mr. Appleton agreed. "And kindly observe Mr. Snarple." Then they both sat speechless.

In the hollow where Mr. Snarple's garden had formerly flourished there now lay a sizable pond, its surface gay with dancing ripples. Here and there the taller clumps of flowers lifted their bright heads above the water. A stone cupid, submerged to the chin, bravely held his sun dial up to the warm sun.

Mr. Snarple, wearing hip boots, was floundering wrathfully about. He seemed to be snatching wet, limp bits of paper from the water.

"What do you suppose he's doing?" Squirt wondered.

"Rescuing love letters, no doubt," Mr. Appleton grinned. "Love letters or — " his voice died away as a sudden suspicion struck him.

The same suspicion occurred to Arthur Amory at exactly the same moment. He had an uneasy memory of many bits of paper floating about the cellar the previous evening.

"There were a lot of papers in the water last night," he said uncomfortably, "in the cellar. Those slips the oil man leaves — and some market slips — "

"All clearly inscribed *A. A. Appleton*," his father murmured. "Do you suppose — "

"General de Gaulle doesn't like Mr. Snarple," Squirt observed thoughtfully. "He doesn't like him at all."

"Naturally," his father agreed. "Who does? The General has excellent taste and is certainly a highly competent engineer, but I do wish he'd thought of those scraps of paper. As I recollect, the oil man's slips are bright yellow and unless I am mistaken

several of those which our neighbor has just salvaged appear to be distinctly yellow in hue."

At this moment Mr. Snarple spied the car and its occupants. Fuming and bellowing, he clambered over the wall and advanced on them, waving the incriminating bits of paper.

"I'll 'ave the Lawr on you for this," he raged. "It's that dirty brat of yours 'as done it, 'im and that animal of 'is, and I've got the evidence right 'ere."

Mr. Appleton dismounted and Squirt, suddenly aware of what a straight and well-set-up man his father really was, was somewhat relieved too.

"My dear sir," Mr. Appleton said icily, "I must inform you that my son is neither a brat nor dirty. Although he is an extremely brilliant young man, no person in his right mind could be so completely idiotic as to believe him capable of placing a large pond in your garden, even with the aid of this fabulous animal, which seems to be a creation of your disordered mentality."

"It's 'im, I tell you," Mr. Snarple shouted, "and I've got the proofs." He shook the wet papers. "Bills, that's wot. Oil bills and market slips and letters, all with your name on 'em. Out of your house — out of your cellar. Your cellar's always being flooded. I've seen it being pumped out and this time you've drained it into my garden. I'm having the Lawr on you — that's wot."

"What you are pleased to call 'the Lawr,' " Mr. Appleton remarked, "may possibly be interested in knowing just how certain of my private, personal papers happen to be in your possession. Beyond that it, or they, will doubtless be quite as bored by your ridiculous ravings as I am. Good day to you — and good fishing."

Mr. Snarple departed, roaring and threatening revenge. Mr. Appleton, about to turn to the car, felt a slight nudge on his ankle and looking down beheld the grinning face of de Gaulle protruding from the ground.

"Why, General," Squirt cried, leaping down, "you're a bad boy. Go home, at once." He stamped three times and de Gaulle sheepishly withdrew.

When they returned from the village, Squirt happily bearing a dozen new arrows, they found Uncle Amory's promised letter waiting. Also the Chief of Police and the First Selectman.

Mr. Appleton, being fairly well acquainted with the two gentlemen, welcomed them pleasantly and introduced his son. De Gaulle, who had received Pearlacy's signal for Trick #40, kept well out of sight.

"If your Dog Warden has left any Scotch, I will be pleased to fix you a highball," Mr. Appleton offered, but the First Selectman refused, to the Chief's obvious disappointment. With little real interest they made known their errand which, of course, concerned Mr. Snarple's complaints.

"Very unfortunate, very unfortunate indeed," Mr. Appleton said. "Nature seems to have been rather unkind to our neighbor. However, with this terrific rain, the contours of the hillside and so forth, it is only to be expected, I suppose."

"He says," said the Selectman, "that there have been worse rains than this and his garden was never flooded before. But I still don't see how you could have had anything to do with it."

"Quite inconceivable, of course," Mr. Appleton agreed heartily.

"That's what I told him," the Chief said. "His garden being down in a hollow like, and with this hill and all and this one of the worst rains we've had in years, what did he expect. Why, half the cellars in town were flooded — "

"Yes," Squirt volunteered, "ours was too. There was a lot of water in it."

"You don't say," said the Chief. "How'd you get rid of it? Got a sump pump, or a drain?"

"Why it seems to have just — seeped out," Mr. Appleton explained, stepping heavily on his son's foot and not apologizing. "Configuration of the land, I suppose. Subsurface strata or something of that sort."

"Then there were all those oil and grocery slips with your name on them," the Selectman dutifully persisted. "He says he found them in the water, but I don't see what that proves."

"Only that the wind blows," Mr. Appleton said. "We have rather tricky winds up here on the hill and Mr. Swain is, perhaps, sometimes a bit careless in removing the trash."

"Sure," agreed the Chief. "That truck of Enoch's scatters garbage and stuff all over town. I've warned him about it a dozen times. That's how come those papers got there."

"Well, we'll send an engine up and pump his garden out," said the Selectman. "I guess that's all we can do for him. Sorry to bother you, Mr. Appleton."

"Not at all, not at all," Mr. Appleton protested pleasantly. "A great pleasure to have seen you; drop in again some time."

So Vigilant Fire Truck #1 arrived and Arthur Amory spent a delightful afternoon observing its operation. The firemen allowed him to put on a helmet and sit on the driver's seat and to present each of them with a pack of his father's cigarettes. Mr. Snarple did not appear.

Chapter 9

SUPPLY AND DEMAND

ON THE TERRACE after dinner Mr. Appleton produced
Uncle Amory's letter. Squirt and General de Gaulle were seated
on the grass, leaning lazily against the stone wall. The General,

who had just finished his dinner of three Bities flakes and two quarts of water, was feeling sleepy and kept trying to nap on Squirt's shoulder.

After the night when he had so nearly starved de Gaulle had increased his portion to three flakes per meal and his rate of growth had increased proportionately. He was now as large as a very large seal. Sitting beside Squirt his head towered several inches above his young master's. The great leathery forepaws were now as large as ping-pong bats.

Mr. Appleton sighed slightly as he eyed the happy pair. "It grieves me to inform you," he said, "that your Uncle's letter contains some startling and not very encouraging news. I do not wish to unduly alarm you, but things do not look too rosy for our stout military friend."

Squirt, who was keeping de Gaulle awake by tickling his nose with a piece of grass, did not seem unduly alarmed and Mrs. Appleton suggested, "You might read the letter."

"So I might," her husband agreed. He put on his glasses and read:

DEAR ARTHUR:

I hope you received my telegram in time and that Arthur Amory managed to rescue every possible flake of the original Bities. As a matter of fact, our analyses proved that they are not Bities at all, but pure, undiluted Vitamin X, a Vitamin of which you have probably never heard (unless you read their silly advertisements) and about which very little is known. It does, however, seem to possess the miraculous, growth-producing power which they claim for it. I have had a conference with the officials of the Bita-Vita Corporation and the general opinion seems to be that through some unaccountable accident of manufacture all the Vitamin X flakes that should have been distributed among several thousand packages of Bities got into one box — that box being the one which, by some chance, ended up in your kitchen.

As you know, these Vitamin X flakes are soft and crumbly. In the ordinary course of manufacture they break up into a fine powder which mixes thoroughly with the other ingredients, only a tiny amount going into each package. Just how this accident happened no one seems to know and it is not especially important.

A rather futile little man named Twigg or Prig or something of the sort, who is in charge of the mixing machine, claimed that such a thing could not possibly have occurred, as he always operates his apparatus with the greatest scientific accuracy. Obviously he is a fool or a liar or both, because it *did* happen.

The sad and alarming fact, however, is this. Vitamin X was developed by and is the sole property of the Bita-Vita Corporation. Its composition is a closely guarded secret and not a flake is available to the public. Since General de Gaulle has grown up on it and seems unable to exist on any other diet I tremble to think what will happen when his present supply is exhausted.

Of course I will bring every possible pressure to bear on the corporation in an effort to force them to release a certain amount for research purposes. In the world of science I possess some influential friends and connections whom I shall use to the utmost to attain this end. The corporation, though, is a most difficult one to deal with. Its officials are men of little vision (beyond profits) — no knowledge of science — and extremely bad manners. My interview with Mr. A. P. Crunch, the president, ended quite unpleasantly.

In the meantime Arthur Amory must conserve his remaining supply most carefully. It might also be wise to experiment with various foods and see if some substitute can be found which General de Gaulle will consider.

Tell Helen that my cold has improved, but I have been forced to have all my clothes altered. The few flakes of Vitamin X which I foolishly tasted produced a total growth of two and one-quarter inches with a corresponding increase in weight. No wonder de Gaulle has attained his present size! With best wishes to you all,

Affectionately,

AMORY

Mr. Appleton folded the letter and returned it to the envelope. Squirt seemed thoughtful, but General de Gaulle yawned loudly, stretched and burrowed his head into Squirt's shoulder.

"Come, Amie," Mrs. Appleton said briskly, "run along up and put de Gaulle to bed and don't worry. I'm sure Amory will arrange something with those horrid Bities people. Or Pearlacy can cook up something he'll like."

Later in the evening Squirt appeared with a pencil, a much-smudged piece of paper and an unhappy air. "I have counted all the flakes that are left," he announced, "and there are just three hundred and forty-five, and a few crumbly ones. With nine a day that means about thirty-eight days."

RL

"Thirty-eight days from now," Mrs. Appleton said, counting on her fingers, "is just about the time you go back to school."

"I hadn't counted on going back this year," he answered. "I thought I'd stay home. How could de Gaulle get along without me?" Tears were plainly imminent.

"The question," Mr. Appleton said, "is not so much how de Gaulle can get along without *you* as how he can get along without Vitamin X. I shall have to put my mind to the problem. In the meantime, go to bed."

During the succeeding weeks he did put his mind to the problem. Squirt also did and Pearlacy put her mind and her best skill to it, all with complete lack of success. She cooked every sort of delectable tidbit that she had ever heard of and several new ones. De Gaulle inspected all these offerings with polite interest and obvious gratitude, but that was as far as he would go.

Finally in desperation Pearlacy consulted a wise woman who lived down by the railroad tracks and invested fifty cents in an unpleasant looking purplish powder which was guaranteed to make anyone eat anything. The powder was to be mixed into a paste, during the dark of the moon, and spread on warm cabbage leaves. All this was done with utmost care, but the General eyed the resulting mess with complete disinterest and this time was scarcely polite in his refusal to touch it. Mr. Appleton repaid Pearlacy her fifty cents.

Uncle Amory too was not idle and wrote frequently to tell of his efforts to secure a supply of vitamin flakes, but his labors seemed just as unsuccessful as Pearlacy's. All the learned scientific societies of which he was a member brought pressure to bear on the Bita-Vita Corporation with no result whatsoever.

Uncle Amory even threatened to make public the ingredients of Bities. "We have analyzed the filthy stuff," he wrote, "and find that the principal ingredients are toasted peanut shells, chopped corn silk and coffee grounds with, of course, an infinitesimal trace of the Vitamin X. I have attempted to blackmail them by threatening to expose their preposterous swindle, but the trouble is they buy so much advertising space that no magazine or newspaper would dare offend them by publishing it, even over my signature.

"However, I will continue to make every effort. Tell Squirt to conserve his present supply as carefully as possible. I hope to come out this week end."

Mrs. Carstairs was seized with a great many sudden inspirations and was constantly appearing with tasty snacks of imported cheese, caviar, truffles, sardines, anchovies and the like, all of which were declined by de Gaulle, but thoroughly appreciated by Mr. Appleton.

The only unperturbed member of the household was de Gaulle himself. He continued to eat his three flakes three times a day with great gusto, washing down each meal with several quarts of water, entirely unmindful of the rapidly dwindling food supply.

After increasing his meals to three flakes his growth became astounding. Soon he was larger than a very large seal; he was rapidly approaching the proportions of a walrus. The successive beds in Squirt's room had now become far too bulky and the General was forced to sleep in the tool house on a pile of straw.

His digging too became a problem, for with his present size

the holes which he made became extremely dangerous, a fact which was pointed out sharply after Mr. Appleton had dropped into one as far as the waist. "I do not wish to be unkind to your little friend," he told Squirt, after he had gotten his wind back, "but he really must use some discretion in his excavating activities. I have no desire, at my age, to be buried alive."

So de Gaulle confined his entrances and exits to two or three well defined holes in out of the way places. This put an end to the submarine and Libby Prison games, but they still had plenty of fun.

The General's sharp nose was wonderfully useful in locating lost arrows; many times he dug out Excalibur or one of the Twelve Apostles from under the matted grass. He also proved adept at singlestick and quarterstaff, looking singularly like a gray robed monk as he stood up on his hind feet and battled furiously. He, of course, was always Friar Tuck, while Squirt varied between being Robin Hood, Little John or Alan a Dale.

They also did a great deal of wrestling. At first, of course, Squirt had been easily able to master his opponent, but as de Gaulle caught up in size they became more evenly matched and now the General had far the best of it. He used his great strength gently, however, sometimes allowing Squirt to win and pin him down. Then, with a slight wriggle de Gaulle would heave up with his powerful forearms, send Squirt flying, tackle him around the ankles and another bout would start.

RL

After these contests they would sprawl lazily in the hot sun for hours doing nothing at all except soaking in air, warmth and contentment — and growing. After his one taste of vitamin flakes, which was never repeated, Squirt's growth continued at a perfectly normal rate. The continual out-of-door games, the wrestling and quarterstaff bouts, had caused him to fill out wonderfully. He was tanned, healthy and overflowing with energy.

"Goodness," said Mrs. Appleton, "de Gaulle has just done wonders for Amie. I've never seen him looking so well."

"He does look much less like a stalk of bleached celery," Mr. Appleton agreed. "We owe the General a great deal and I dread the day when his food supply will give out."

"Oh, I'm sure Amory can arrange something," she said; "let's not cross that bridge till we come to it."

"It will prove more than a Bridge of Sighs when we do," he said gloomily. "There will be woe and lamentation and a wail-

ing by the shore. Pearlacy too; she is devoted to him. There will be tears in the soup for a week and I hate tears in the soup."

"Oh well, she never does salt it enough anyway," Mrs. Appleton said. "Cheer up now and try to think of something pleasant. Amory is coming out for the week end and perhaps we can have a good game of bridge."

Mr. Appleton gave her a stony glare. "If *that's* your idea of something pleasant," he snorted, and went to his study to do some typing.

When Uncle Amory arrived he gave a dramatic account of his various interviews with the Bities executives. He was bristling with indignation and his recital was so long and violent that bridge was never mentioned.

"The National Zoological Society has taken the matter up," he concluded, "and they may be able to accomplish something, but I doubt it. Preposterous situation, simply preposterous. Impossible people to deal with, perfectly impossible. Ought to be thrown in jail."

"On a diet of Bities and water," Mr. Appleton added.

"And carpet tacks," suggested Squirt, starting sadly off for bed.

Sunday afternoon Mr. Appleton, Squirt and Uncle Amory were seated on the hillside in the shade of a maple tree where they hoped there might be a breeze. The August sun was blistering hot and the breeze had not materialized. De Gaulle had gone down one of his holes which was close by and had been absent some time.

The conversation was languid, Mr. Appleton was half dozing and Uncle Amory had quite exhausted himself with his diatribes against the Bities Corporation and all its works.

Suddenly Squirt started and gave a sharp cry, "Uncle Amory, look!"

Uncle Amory looked and gave an even sharper exclamation as something green and striped slowly began to emerge from de Gaulle's entrance hole. Mr. Appleton, waking and beholding this large object, which looked startlingly like an enormous serpent, leaped wildly to his feet and tripped over Uncle Amory's outstretched legs.

"Good grief," he choked. "What is it?"

Slowly and deliberately the mysterious object continued to rise into the sunlight, then rolled out on the grass — a long, striped watermelon! It was followed by the smiling countenance of General de Gaulle.

"Amazing! Amazing!" exploded Uncle Amory.

He reached out and rolled the melon over to him. He lifted it up and smelled it, pressed the ends and then rapped it with practiced knuckles. "A watermelon," he finally pronounced, "and as splendid a specimen as I have seen in years. Dead ripe too, if I am not mistaken. Squirt, do you possess a knife?"

Squirt handed over his Boy Scout knife; Uncle Amory deftly split the melon and carved three large slices.

"You may not realize it," he went on, settling back contentedly, "but in the prime of my youth I was the champion watermelon eater of the county. If you young amateurs will give close attention I shall now demonstrate some of the finer points of watermelon eating."

Mr. Appleton and Squirt paid little attention to the finer points. They were more interested in the juicy, dripping sweetness of their own portions. Squirt popped seeds at de Gaulle, who happily batted them back with his paddle-like paws.

"But — isn't it stealing, really?" Squirt asked, as he finished his first slice and reached for another.

"Stealing? Preposterous, absurd," cried Uncle Amory, who was well into his second. "A direct gift from the gods (just which ones I cannot guess) through the generous medium of our stalwart General."

"I have a feeling," said Mr. Appleton, cutting himself another slice, "that this particular donor is our quite ungodlike neighbor, Mr. Snarple. As far as I know he is the only person in this locality who attempts to raise watermelons."

"He is," Squirt said. "Pearlacy said that he raises a special

prize kind. He starts them in the greenhouse and sets them out later. She says that her boy friend has peeked over the wall and watched them quite a lot."

"A pleasant occupation," observed Uncle Amory, "but tantalizing, I should think." He cut the remainder of the melon into three grossly unequal slices and helped himself to the largest.

"I should like to watch the General at work. It is really a scientific point which should be observed. Also I think that Helen and Pearlacy would appreciate a taste of these delicious fruits. Moreover, Sunday is Pearlacy's boy friend's evening to call and he should have some reward for all those hours of loving vigil. In short, nephew, we must have another."

Mr. Appleton refused to stir and the south meadow was forbidden to Squirt. De Gaulle, however, when their wish was made known, eagerly scrambled down his hole and Uncle Amory, a bit unsteadily, made his way down the hill to the wall of the Snarple garden.

Whatever his other faults, Mr. Snarple was a good gardener. Uncle Amory, peering over the wall, was forced to admire the luxuriant flower beds, the neatly trimmed grass plots and brick-edged walks, all recovered from the flooding of the early summer. He admired also the orderly vegetable garden which lay beyond, on a slight rise of ground.

Along the near edge of this was the watermelon bed, its lovely fruit basking in the sunshine. Uncle Amory's contemplation of the pleasant scene was suddenly blotted out by the not pleasant face of Mr. Snarple less than three feet from his own. Mr. Snarple had been weeding a bed directly below the wall; straightening up had brought them face to face.

Uncle Amory was first to recover from the surprise and spoke amiably. "Good afternoon, good afternoon, pleasant day, pleasant day," he said. Mr. Snarple glowered.

"Just admiring your garden," Uncle Amory went on hastily. "Splendid, splendid! Beautifully kept. Gorgeous flowers, gorgeous; and magnificent vegetables, simply magnificent."

Mr. Snarple thawed slightly and grumbled. "Could be better if there wasn't so many thieves and vandals about. Floods and stealing and breakage going on all the time."

"You don't say," Uncle Amory clucked sympathetically. "My, my. Unfortunate, unfortunate. By George! Aren't those watermelons? How did you ever manage that in this climate? Remarkable, remarkable."

As Mr. Snarple, thawing still more, gazed proudly on his prize melons, the very largest one gently upended itself and began to settle into the earth. As it disappeared, the vine dragging after it, a broad paw suddenly appeared and great claws neatly snipped off the stem. Mr. Snarple with a howl rushed frantically over to the bed, but there was only a clean, round, melon-sized hole in the ground.

"My, my," said Uncle Amory, departing hastily. "One of the most amazing instances of capillary attraction I have ever witnessed. Quite amazing, quite."

When he reached the maple tree up the hill General de Gaulle and the watermelon had just arrived.

"Squirt," said Uncle Amory. "That first one seemed to me just a trifle warm. I think that if we put this one in the spring it should reach a really perfect temperature by about nine or nine-thirty this evening. You are invited."

Mr. Appleton, who had gone to sleep again, didn't say anything.

Chapter 10

SHE BLOWS!

SO THE HOT DAYS of August passed, while de Gaulle
grew and grew. The only shadow sometimes darkening the days
was the steadily decreasing supply of vitamin flakes. August
passed into September, the evenings grew cool, the scent of

burning leaves was always on the air. The time for the return to school was drawing close, but no decision had been made on Squirt's plea to remain at home.

The General, although still amiable and lovable as ever, had gradually acquired more independence of movement. His disappearances underground became longer; often he failed to respond to Squirt's signals to return. More and more frequently Squirt, racing out to the tool house after breakfast, would find the General's bed unoccupied and the General gone, perhaps not to return for a day or two.

That he went far afield was made clear on several occasions.

One morning a whole Boy Scout Troop, accompanied by several scoutmasters, two policemen and several heavily armed hunters tramped through the south field. Inquiry brought the startling news that a bear had been seen by an old lady who lived a mile or so away across the valley. Squirt, of course, went along.

The old lady was in quite a state, but positive that she had seen a bear. Later, she was less positive that it was a bear, but sure that she had seen *something*. It had been the size of a bear, had dark gray fur, but seemed an odd shape. It had hastily gone into the ground when she screamed.

The Boy Scouts eventually located the hole, but no one cared to explore it. So the hunters shot their guns down it, the policemen tossed in a couple of tear gas bombs, the photographers from the *Eastporter-Herald* photographed it, the old lady and the hunters. Squirt stayed discreetly in the background.

When he returned home de Gaulle was sleeping soundly in the tool house. The General woke up, asked for breakfast and consumed it eagerly, entirely undisturbed by Squirt's scolding. Then he went to sleep again and slumbered all afternoon.

A few nights later a car was wrecked on a road a half mile or so from the Appleton home. The driver was not injured, but considerably shaken by what he thought he had seen crossing the road. At first he maintained that it was a giant panda; after a while he decided that it had been a crocodile; in the police court he admitted that, after all, it might have been a cow. Since it was proven that on the night of the accident he had left a tavern in a somewhat exhilarated state, the judge fined him five dollars and costs. But Squirt knew that de Gaulle had been out that night and gave him another sharp talking to. The General accepted it amiably and then went to sleep, not especially repentant.

Another time there was a great deal of noise and excitement when Mr. Snarple dropped into a hole in his garden; a hole so deep that had he not been holding a rake at the time there is no knowing where he might have dropped to. Squirt did not reprove de Gaulle very strongly for this escapade.

Eventually there came a day when the bottom of the Bities box was barely covered with a scattering of vitamin flakes, and these mostly crumbly ones. Squirt, counting them sadly, reckoned it to be about a four days' supply. This was also the moment when something definite must be decided about the return to school, but no one seemed able to decide anything definite about that.

In the afternoon Uncle Amory arrived for the week end. He could not help much in making any decision either, and seemed quite depressed. His Paper was to be read in about two weeks, before the International Convention of Zoological Societies. He had planned to have General de Gaulle brought in for a personal appearance. The Zoo had promised to provide a truck and of course Squirt and the family were to go, too. Mrs. Appleton was contemplating a new hat for the occasion. But with only a four-day supply of food on hand the chances for de Gaulle's personal appearance seemed slim.

In fact, everything seemed dubious, uncertain and depressing, even the weather. The lovely mellowness of September had suddenly turned hot and heavy, the sky threatened rain. Lunch had not been at all what it should have been; Pearlacy's boy friend was cutting up and she was in the dumps.

The General had been absent for a day and a half. Squirt had spent most of the day up on the hill pounding out signals and orders with the spade, without getting any response. Tired, discouraged and dirty he now joined the others on the terrace.

"De Gaulle just won't come," he said, wearily. "I've tried S.O.S. and number 38 and even 454 — that's a very special emergency signal — but he won't come. I'm sure he would if he knew Uncle Amory were here. He's learned a new trick for you, Uncle Amory, the same one he used to do with a tennis ball only now he uses a big round stone. He doesn't toss it to me though, because it's so heavy I can't even lift it. It would be very dangerous."

"Amie, you're terribly dirty," Mrs. Appleton interrupted. "Suppose you run and get a bath and tell Pearlacy chocolate soufflé for dessert."

"I don't think I need a *complete* bath," Squirt said, "but I'll tell Pearlacy. It won't be very good though. Her boy friend has broken her heart and owes her twelve dollars."

He dragged off toward the kitchen just as Mrs. Carstairs arrived.

She was carrying a small can which she gave to Mrs. Appleton. "I just found these on the very top shelf of the closet," she cried. "They're marrons, Helen, the real old-fashioned kind. Heaven knows how long we've had them, but I'm just sure de Gaulle would like them. At least we could try. Of course you can't get them now, so even if he did like them it wouldn't do much good, would it? I mean one can wouldn't go very far, would it?"

"No," said Mr. Appleton.

"My, it's hot," Mrs. Carstairs sighed, settling herself. "Wouldn't anyone like to go to the beach?"

"What for?" asked Mr. Appleton.

"Oh, a swim or something. Someone said the water was nice and warm for September."

"No," said Uncle Amory.

Then for a long time no one said anything. Mr. and Mrs. Appleton were wondering what to decide about Squirt's going back to school and what would happen when de Gaulle's food gave out. Uncle Amory was thinking about his Paper and his speech. Mrs. Carstairs wasn't thinking about anything special except how hot it was and wondering if anyone would remember to close the windows if it rained.

There was a low rumbling and Mrs. Appleton said, "I'm sure it is going to rain; that's the third time I've heard thunder."

"I am too," Mrs. Carstairs agreed. "I do hope someone closes the windows. It doesn't sound like ordinary thunder though. Perhaps it's blasting or something. It may be that new highway they are building. Don't you think it sounds like blasting, Arthur?"

"No," said Mr. Appleton — and then for another long time no one said anything, while the air grew hotter and heavier. The low dark clouds rolled steadily in from the south and now and then the rumbling occurred. It really didn't sound exactly like thunder; the jarring seemed to come from the earth rather than the sky.

Arthur Amory reappeared, somewhat bathed, but languid. He slumped down on the terrace and announced "I've made a poem about the President of the Bita-Vita Corporation. Would anyone like to hear it?"

"No," Mr. Appleton said.

"It goes like this:

> A. P. Crunch
> Is a dunce,
> I'd like to punch
> His nose just once."

"Why limit yourself?" Uncle Amory asked, sleepily. "I should make it ten times at least."

"It wouldn't rhyme," Squirt answered. "I told Pearlacy about the soufflé. She was crying, but I don't know whether about her boy friend or de Gaulle."

Mrs. Carstairs decided that she'd better telephone home and remind someone about the windows if it rained and then she decided that someone would probably attend to them anyway, besides it might not rain.

About this time the rumbling suddenly increased in violence.

134

It became an almost continuous jarring, boiling, grumbling sound. The ground seemed to shudder. The glasses on the table rattled and several apples dropped from the tree, one on Mr. Appleton.

Everyone had sprung up and Mrs. Carstairs cried, "Goodness gracious, what *is* it, an earthquake or atoms or what?"

"It sounds," said Mr. Appleton, rubbing his head, "as though Mother Earth were having an extremely violent attack of indigestion." And it did sound exactly like that.

Pearlacy came flying around the corner of the house, spread her arms wide and declaimed, "The Lord God is speaking in His Heaven. Let all the earth keep silence before him." Then she flopped down on her knees and began to pray.

"Preposterous, absurd," Uncle Amory shouted. "Heaven's nothing to do with it. It's coming from the earth. Slight subsidence of some sort, doubtless."

Whatever it was, the rumbling, boiling, grumbling sound became still louder. Several more apples fell and Pearlacy prayed even more fervently. Mrs. Carstairs wondered if she shouldn't hurry home to see about the windows.

Then, when the noise seemed to have reached a climax, Squirt suddenly yelped, "Look, look! Down in the low field!"

Down in the low field, several hundred yards from where they stood, a huge eruption seemed to be taking place. There was a great burst of vapor, then a billowing cloud of blackness, shot

through with jets of steam. A shower of stones, mud, shrubs, clods of earth rose as though from an exploding land mine. The roar was like the explosion of a Gargantuan boiler. Higher and higher the black geyser rose.

Then, shooting up from the center of it, for a moment they clearly saw the great form of General de Gaulle. He seemed to float up gently, almost like something in a slow motion picture.

He was turning over and over, his big flipper-like front paws
making easy strokes as though swimming.

Up and up he went; up and up and over and over, until at last
he melted into the low scudding dark clouds. Once or twice

through openings in the clouds they caught glimpses of his dark form, still rising slowly, still swimming easily.

Squirt gave one loud wail, "De Gaulle!" but the others were speechless for some time.

Then Mrs. Appleton cried, "Shouldn't we telephone someone, the Police or the Fire Department or something?"

"I suppose so," Mr. Appleton said dazedly. "And perhaps the Bureau of Missing Moles."

Things began to happen immediately. The field where the eruption was taking place was close to the main road. Cars stopped and blew their horns. People could be seen running in circles. Then the wail of sirens began; the big alarm siren in the village, the rising crescendo of fire engine sirens, police car sirens, ambulance sirens, all converging.

Mrs. Carstairs sniffed the air. "You know," she said, "it smells exactly the way it did when our oil burner blew up. Sort of oily."

It did indeed. They could all recognize distinctly a heavy odor of oil. The great billowing geyser had now subsided. There was only an occasional outburst of gas, mud and water. The rumbling had died away, but in the center of the low field a black fountain spurted heavily and steadily.

"Of course it's oily," snapped Uncle Amory. "It *is* oil. Haven't you ever seen a gusher brought in?"

"Of course not," answered Mrs. Carstairs. "Why should I?"

The sirens grew louder. Squirt, recognizing Vigilant Truck #1, raced down the hill to greet it. Then people began to arrive. The First, Second and Third Selectmen were suddenly there, the Fire Chief, the Police Chief and even Mr. Snodgrass, the Dog Warden.

The State Police kept everyone away from the rapidly spreading pool and allowed no smoking. The First Selectman telephoned to the Road Department to send out a couple of bulldozers and gave orders that they were to throw up a dam to contain the oil.

Everyone in town whom the Appletons knew seemed to arrive at once and all gathered on the terrace. Mrs. Appleton sent Pearlacy for ice and glasses and set Mr. Appleton to bringing out more chairs. Mrs. Carstairs told everyone how she had been just about to go home and see about the windows when *it* had happened, and just how it had all sounded and looked.

Enoch Swain rolled up in his garbage truck to see if there was anything he could do and later Pearlacy's boy friend arrived. In the excitement of the moment their tiff was forgotten, he paid her back four of the owed twelve dollars and the prospects for dinner seemed brighter, if things ever calmed down.

They didn't, very much.

The reporters and photographers came and asked foolish questions and blinded everyone with flashlights. Mrs. Carstairs refused to be photographed until she had sent home for a different hat and Uncle Amory became enraged because one reporter kept spelling his name *Emery*.

Then the engineers from the Oil Company came and later there arrived trucks and machinery and lots of workmen to cap the well. This took all night and most of the next day and of course no one slept. Pearlacy and her boy friend made gallons of coffee for the oil men and for anyone else who wanted it, one of whom, strangely enough, was Mr. Snarple, from next door.

Later there were phone calls from the Chamber of Commerce, the Department of the Interior and the Governor of the State. They were all greatly excited because this was the first time that oil had been found within eight hundred miles of this locality. They asked a great many questions, and as Mr. Appleton did not care to mention de Gaulle he could not explain how or why it had all happened. He finally became tired and turned the telephone over to Mrs. Carstairs.

Next day the engineers and lawyers of the Oil Company came and talked all afternoon about leases and options and royalties and other things that Mr. Appleton couldn't make head or tail of and in which Squirt was not at all interested. He would much rather have watched the workmen.

Mr. and Mrs. Appleton decided that the well really should belong to Squirt, so all the papers were made out to Arthur Amory Appleton. One of the lawyers said that it was customary to name every well and Squirt said he wanted this one named *The*

General de Gaulle #1, so it was put down that way in all the documents.

At the mention of the General, Squirt's lip began to quiver, but just then one of the other lawyers mentioned the sum which the royalties would probably produce every month and Mrs. Appleton promptly fainted. In the resulting confusion Squirt's sorrow was forgotten.

Those first few days were so filled with various excitements that no one had much time to mourn the General's departure. There was the capping of the well and the signing of all the papers. Vigilant Truck #1 stood by for a couple of days in case of fire and Squirt became most intimate with the crew who came up to the house at all hours for coffee. Then the Oil Company sent a pumper and tank trucks to clean out the pool of oil and later pumps and machinery and pipes came for pumping from the well. This machinery was all housed in a neat little building and when everything was all straightened up it did not look at all objectionable.

It had been decided that Squirt was to return to school, to which he was now quite agreeable. Mr. and Mrs. Appleton were to drive him up and the station wagon was all packed, for they were to make an early start next morning. Squirt's skis and bow were tied up under the roof, Excalibur, Daniel Boone and the Twelve Apostles carefully stowed away under one of the seats.

Up in his room Squirt was doing last minute packing before going to bed. He was being assisted by Pearlacy who was sniffling slightly, as she always did when Squirt went back to school. She was holding the Bities box with its few remaining flakes.

"Yessuh," she promised, "I shore will take good care of these. Casen he *should* come back he'll be mighty hongry. I don't reckon he ever will though. Well anyhow, I guess you'll be the very richest young gentman in that whole school. Ain't many young gentmen owns a oil well all to hisself."

"I guess maybe I will be," Squirt said sadly. "But I'd rather have de Gaulle. He was a very interesting pet." Pearlacy burst into tears and left.

Everything was packed now, his teeth were brushed, his alarm clock set. Arthur Amory sat down and read "The Book of Interesting Tricks" from beginning to end. He sniffled a good deal over some of them, especially those about licking his fingers and acting as a muffler.

Then he wiped his eyes, blew his nose and carefully wrote:

#*50. To Discover an Oil Well.*
The last Trick of all.

FINNIS.

RL

18 7284 16 P
#3